TO MARRY AN HEIRESS

TO MARRY AN HEIRESS

Julia Parks

THORNDIKE

CHIVERS

This Large Print edition is published by Thorndike Press®, Waterville, Maine USA and by BBC Audiobooks, Ltd, Bath, England.

Published in 2003 in the U.S. by arrangement with Zebra Books, an imprint of Kensington Publishing Corp.

Published in 2003 in the U.K. by arrangement with Kensington Publishing Corp.

U.S. Hardcover 0-7862-5861-6 (Romance)
U.K. Hardcover 0-7540-7394-7 (Chivers Large Print)

The text of this Large Print edition is unabridged.
Other aspects of the book may vary from the original edition.

Set in 16 pt. Plantin by Minnie B. Raven.

Printed in the United States on permanent paper.

British Library Cataloguing-in-Publication Data available

Library of Congress Cataloging-in-Publication Data

Parks, Julia.
    To marry an heiress / Julia Parks.
      p. cm.
    ISBN 0-7862-5861-6 (lg. print : hc : alk. paper)
    1. Administration of estates — Fiction.   2. London
(England) — Fiction.   3. Country homes — Fiction.
4. Large type books.   I. Title.
PS3616.A756T6 2003
    813′.6—dc22   2003059295

I dedicate this book to Grandbaby number three whose publication year is the same as this novel.

One

"Montgomery, I want a word with you and your brothers."

"Papa, surely it can wait. Can you not see that Mrs. Richland is here?"

"Know you'll excuse us, madam," said Viscount Tavistoke, toddling across the faded carpet and taking this lady's hand to help her rise.

"Papa!" exclaimed the young man, leaping to his feet.

"Please think nothing of it, Mr. Darby. I would not dream of intruding when your father wants to speak to you," said Mrs. Richland.

"Thank you, dear Mrs. Richland," said the younger man. He offered his arm as they walked out of the drawing room toward the front door. "You are always so accommodating. Shall I see you tomorrow night at the assembly?"

"Certainly, I will be there. You know Jeremy enjoys seeing his parishioners enjoying themselves." The matron smiled smugly as he bowed over her hand with a kiss before handing her up into the small dogcart pulled by a broken-down bay mare.

A slight smile curved his lips as the man watched his visitor drive away. Then, recalling his father's indecorous summons, the honorable Montgomery Darby grimaced and returned to the drawing room where his father paced back and forth.

"Papa, I resent your dismissing Mrs. Richland in such a cavalier manner. She is a guest in our home, and . . ."

"I fail to see why you would resent it, my boy. The woman is as dull as ditchwater and not a bit prettier than her personality," said the older man, his laughter dissolving into a hacking cough.

Taking in his father's rumpled appearance and less than appealing odor, his son accused, "You have been gambling again."

"And drinking and smoking a pipe, and having a damn fine time of it, too, except . . . but never mind all that. Where the devil are those brothers of yours? I sent for them more than ten minutes ago."

"It is not raining, so Max is almost certainly on horseback somewhere in Cornwall, and Tristram is no doubt settled in some out of the way spot in the house, drawing, or writing his poetry."

"Demmed waste of a man, if you ask me
. . . being a poet!"

"Isn't it a good thing, Papa, that no one
asked you," said his youngest son, slipping
into the room. The long-legged young man
crossed the room and plopped down on
one of the chairs by the fire. He opened his
ever-present sketchbook and applied his
pencil to it in swift, broad strokes. His
blond hair fell across his face, hiding it
from view.

"It's just that . . ." began Lord Tavistoke,
only to be interrupted again.

"What the devil is it this time, Papa?"
said his second son, striding into the room
in his riding gear, switching a crop against
his leg.

Viscount Tavistoke glared at each of his
three sons in turn. His youngest, Tristram,
had his late wife's blond hair and dreamy
blue eyes. Then came Max — dark hair
and blue eyes, he was a hell-raiser like his
father, thought the viscount, throwing out
his chest with pride. And finally, the eldest,
Montgomery, who was watching him politely. He had the same dark hair as his
twin, Max, but his eyes were dark too. He
was a good boy. They all were, thought
Viscount Tavistoke, tears coming to his
eyes. He dashed them away angrily.

"Papa, what has happened?" asked Montgomery, forgetting his previous annoyance over his father's dismissal of his friend.

"What? Oh, nothing, nothing at all. Pay no attention to me. I sometimes get sentimental — all old men do."

"You are hardly old, Papa," said Max. "By my calculations, you are only nine-and-fifty."

"I feel much older," said their father, again looking at each of them in turn. The twins were nearing thirty, and Tristram was only five years younger. And they were handsome, each in his own way. Shaking the years from his shoulders, the viscount smiled. "Besides, I have a solution to my ails."

As if driven by one mind, each of his sons' left brows shot up. When their father beamed at them like that, it could only mean one thing — he was up to something.

"I have a proposition for you, boys."

"Papa, I do wish you would remember that we are not boys anymore. Monty and I are eight-and-twenty, and Tris is, what — three-and-twenty." Max leaned against a table, crossing his booted feet and his arms to show that he was not interested in anything his dissolute father might have to offer.

"Very well then, I have a proposition for my three ancient sons. Do you want to hear it or not?"

Coming to attention, Max glared at his father. Montgomery signaled his brother to be patient. With a shrug of his broad shoulders, Max subsided.

"Good. What about you, Tristram? Are you listening?"

His son looked up from his sketchbook, where he was sketching his once-handsome father. He shrugged his slim shoulders and put down his pencil.

"Very well then, here it is. I want the three of you to go to London for the Season and secure brides for yourselves," said the viscount.

"The devil you say!"

"Must be dicked in the nob!"

"No!"

This last succinct response came from his heir, Montgomery, just as the viscount had suspected it might. Ignoring this, he turned to his other sons.

"I am prepared to offer each of you those estates — you know which ones. They are small, but they each have a house."

"They each have a crumbling shack, more like, Papa," commented Max.

"Still, it would be a home, and you know I have nothing else to offer. All the rest is entailed to Montgomery — an entail, I might add, that has yet to be renewed."

" 'All the rest,' " murmured Tristram, glancing around at the cracked plaster and threadbare furnishings.

"If you don't wish to comply with my wishes, I will be forced to sell both of those estates."

"To pay more gambling debts?" said Montgomery, in a recriminating tone. "How could you do that to your own sons? Those estates have been promised to them all their lives. It was arranged by Grand-father's solicitor when you and Mother were wed."

"Yes, yes, but that was long ago, and my solicitor has found a way out of it. Trouble is, the way they stand now, nobody would pay me for them."

"How delightful, Max, to know we are being promised estates of absolutely no value," said Tristram, ignoring the glare his father sent his way. He bent over his sketchbook once more, the strokes coming fast and sure.

"Not worthless. Only in need of care,

Tristram," said his eldest brother. "You and Max could make something of them, if you would only try."

"You mean that if the estates belonged to them, they might make something of them," said the viscount, his eyes narrowing as he studied his younger sons. "Trouble is, you need money to make anything of them. And that's why I propose that you go to London. I am even willing to sign over the titles of the estates . . . provided, of course, you manage to win suitable brides."

"Papa, why the devil should either Tris or myself want a wife? I mean, Monty needs to marry to get himself an heir, but he already has his sights set on Mrs. Richland."

"Here now! No need to bandy about such a rumor," said Montgomery.

"Anyway, Monty is the only one who needs an heir, not Tris or I."

"Not just any wife, Max. You must all be careful of your choices. You must wed heiresses. It is the only way to recoup the family finances," said their father.

The twins gaped at him, but quiet Tristram said, "Ah, now we get to the crux of the matter."

"Well, you would not wish to forget your

sire when you have secured your good fortune. Moreover, I have arranged for your journey and have secured the help of my friend, the Marquess of Cravenwell. He has generously agreed to fund your stay while you are in London. Therefore, it is only right that I should share in your good fortune."

"I think the entire scheme is reprehensible," said Montgomery.

"Then you're a young fool," snapped his father. "I am not asking you to do anything every other parent does not ask. Do you think there is any father who sends his child into the marriage mart saying, 'Catch yourself a pauper'?"

"Of course not, Papa, but must we be so mercenary about it?"

"Yes, Tristram, you must, and in return, you and Maxwell will receive those small patches of land from your mother's dowry. The trouble is, the cottages on them are little more than hovels. If you ever hope to have a family, you'll need more than a fistful of the ready to bring those cottages up to snuff."

"I don't think the dowry exists that would suffice for that," grumbled Max, twitching his riding crop against his boot.

"Nonsense, my boy. There are fortunes

to be had in London. You're all handsome lads. A bit of flirtation and each of you could find yourselves well-breeched for life. What do you say?" he asked, smiling at each of his sons.

The twins still hesitated, but the fair-haired Tristram surprised him. Rising from the tattered leather chair, he said, "I'll do it, Papa. If nothing else, I think a writer should see a bit of the world, and up to now, my world has been very limited."

"That's my boy," said his sire, beaming at his youngest son. "And you, Max? You are always ready to accept a dare. Will you dare to leave your horses behind and try your hand at gentling one of the fairer sex?"

Max grinned at his father. Taking in the hopeful, bloodshot eyes, he said, "Why not? Like Tristram, I have a desire to see what London has to offer. It has become dashed dull around here."

"Excellent!" said the viscount, rubbing his hands together gleefully. Then, turning to his heir, who continued to glare at him, he said, "Let me speak to Montgomery alone, boys." Obediently, his two younger sons left the room, leaving Viscount Tavistoke alone with his heir.

"What do you really hope to gain from all this, Papa?"

"Me? I will not lie to you, Montgomery. You must admit, I have never lied to any of you boys." A grunt was the only response he received, so the viscount continued, "I want to see all of you boys settled. That is first and foremost in my mind. I know I have been less than responsible when it comes to providing a suitable inheritance for each of you — even you, Montgomery. I mean, I hardly consider Darwood Hall a suitable inheritance for the future Viscount Tavistoke."

"It is all I ever hoped for, Papa. All I ever wanted. You know that."

"Yes, but what can you do with it? I know you want to make improvements to the land, to try some of those new farming methods. I see and hear more than you think, my boy."

"I have managed to do pretty well so far. I shall continue to manage," said Montgomery proudly.

"How? By wedding the likes of Mrs. Richland? All she has to bring to a marriage is that whining, skinny son of hers."

"Papa, I'll not have you . . ."

"Maligning your lady love? Of course not, Montgomery. But let me ask you, do you really love her? If you do, I'll not say another word against her. Is it really love, or is it that she is simply convenient?"

His son's handsome face was drawn into a frown, but he remained silent, and the viscount saw his opportunity.

"This is your chance, Montgomery, your chance to make something of Darwood Hall. You can make it everything you ever wanted it to be. Go to London and find yourself a suitable and wealthy mistress for the Hall."

"I don't know."

"Then allow me to tell you, Montgomery. You have been holding this place together with the sweat of your brow and a prayer. Now you have a chance to secure your future and that of your brothers, because with this estate, you are the one most likely to find success. Once you are wed, you will be in a position to help your brothers. I'm not asking you to wed a dragon, my boy, just some suitable young lady who possesses a decent dowry."

"Perhaps."

"What's more, my boy, I need you to go and look after Max and Tristram. You know what they are. Tristram always has his head in the clouds, just like your dear mother did. And Max? He's just as fool-hardy as his father," he said with a self-deprecating chuckle. Laying his hand on

Montgomery's shoulder, he said softly, "You're the one with his head screwed on right and tight. I need you to keep an eye on them. Will you do that for me?"

Dark brown eyes met and held for a moment before the honorable Montgomery Darby dropped his gaze and made his decision.

"Very well, Papa. I will go to London and do my best to keep Max and Tristram out of trouble while finding myself a nice, amenable heiress."

"I knew I could count on you, my boy!"

"Clarissa, fetch my pink shawl, won't you?"

"The pink one? I would have thought the yellow would . . ."

"I said the pink, dear. Pray do not be so foolish as to question my sense of fashion," said the golden-haired beauty as she rolled her china blue eyes, causing her male entourage to chuckle. "One has only to look at that brown gown and realize you should leave all decisions about fashion to me."

As her cousin Clarissa made her way from the tasteful drawing room, she heard the squeaky-voiced Mr. Phelps say, "Everyone knows your sense of fashion is impeccable, Miss Landis."

18

"La, you are too kind, sir," she replied, favoring the young man with a languishing glance. "Oh, Clarissa."

Clarissa settled a smile on her face before poking her head around the doorway and saying sweetly, "Yes, Adele?"

"Make sure you bring me the matching handkerchief and parasol."

"Of course, Adele."

Clarissa Starnes made her way up the stairs and down the hall to her cousin's room. Opening the door, she shook her head, just as she always did, over the profusion of pink in the lavishly furnished boudoir. The pink shawl was draped over a pink velvet upholstered chaise-longue. The handkerchief her cousin also required was not in the drawer where it was usually to be found. Frowning, Clarissa pulled the bell rope and waited patiently for her cousin's maid to arrive.

Picking up the ivory comb from the dressing table, Clarissa raked it through her dark, straight locks. Closing her eyes, she could imagine her mother's gentle touch as she brushed the long tresses before threading a silk ribbon through them. She had always ended the process with a gentle kiss on Clarissa's brow.

The door opened, and Clarissa dabbed

the single tear from the corner of her eye before turning to face Bates, Adele's dragon of a maid.

Nose in the air, the servant asked, "Did you ring for me, miss?"

"Yes, Bates. Your mistress wants her pink handkerchief to match her pink shawl. I looked, but I could not . . ."

"Th' handkerchiefs are in this drawer now. But what does Miss Landis want with th' pink shawl? It won't do at all with the gown she is wearing this afternoon."

"I couldn't say. I only told her that I would fetch them," said Clarissa, taking the proffered handkerchief, picking up the shawl and parasol, edging toward the door, and making good her escape.

"That girl wouldn't know fashion from a turnip in the garden," muttered the dragon.

Clarissa, whose hearing was quite good, grinned and stored away that particular description of her cousin for later on — for one of those times when Adele's temper flashed, leaving Clarissa feeling sadly bruised. She would trot out that comment — not to Adele's face, of course — and she would feel better.

In the past ten years, whenever Clarissa was feeling very alone and very insignificant, it always helped to know that she was not the only one who thought her perfectly beautiful cousin was not quite so perfect after all.

Not that Adele Landis was a terrible person, or that Clarissa's life with her Uncle Clarence and Aunt Frances was horrible. When her aunt sent Adele out to refurbish her wardrobe before the Season began, she had sent Clarissa right along with her. Clarissa, of course, had been very conservative in her choices, while Adele, the indulged daughter, had been extravagant. But that was how things were supposed to be. If it had been Adele whose parents had perished at sea instead of hers, Clarissa felt certain their roles would have been reversed.

"Oh, there you are, Miss Starnes. Your cousin sent me to look for you," said Lord Grant, a handsome young man whose financial situation made his pursuit of her cousin quite impossible. But he was always kind, and Clarissa smiled at him.

"Do you have them?" he asked urgently.

Clarissa held out the shawl and handkerchief, and he took them from her and scurried back to her cousin's side, carefully placing the shawl about Adele's narrow shoulders as if she were the Madonna herself.

Clarissa shrugged and propped the parasol against the doorjamb. Then she returned to her seat near the window where she could watch the comings and goings of their neighbors as well as utilize the afternoon light to see the tiny stitches on the chair cover she was making.

Holding two hanks of green wool up to the sunlight, she frowned. The lighter color was prettier for the foliage around daisies she was stitching, but the darker one . . . Clarissa dropped the skeins of wool and leaned forward, her mouth sagging open.

"Whatever is the matter with you, Clarissa? Here is Porter with the tea tray. You must come and pour out," said Adele, rising and floating across the room to stand with her hands on her hips, between Clarissa and the sight which held her captive.

Clarissa shifted to see past Adele's hips.

"What in the world?" began Adele, twisting to discover why Clarissa was staring so. "Oh, so that is . . . my, what broad shoulders!"

By now, the entire assemblage was gathered at the window, staring shamelessly at three young men who had descended from a hackney cab and were standing on the pavement, paying the driver.

"Have you ever seen them before?" asked Clarissa.

"Never. Look like three country simpletons to me," said Mr. Pitchly, his nose in the air.

"Hardly the sort of people who could actually afford to live in this quarter of the city," said Lord Grant, watching Adele's shining eyes.

"One can never tell," murmured Adele, licking her lips. "If they are just come from the country, they will not have had time to purchase suitable wardrobes."

"Whose house is that?" asked Lord Grant.

"The Marquess of Cravenwell," said Clarissa, wishing she could sink through the carpet.

"There you have it. They cannot be suitable if they are related to the dirty marquess," said Mr. Pitchly with a sneer.

At that moment, the tallest of the trio happened to glance their way. Adele, with her golden hair and shining blue eyes, nodded regally in reply to his bow.

Clarissa sat back and carefully put away her needlework before slipping out of her chair. In the hall, she motioned to the Landis butler.

"Porter, please send for Miss Anderson to pour out. I . . . I have the headache of a sudden and feel unequal to the task."

"Of course, miss." The kindly butler snapped his fingers, and a footman leapt forward. "Fetch Miss Anderson at once. I believe she is in the library."

"Yes, sir."

"Shall I lend you my arm, Miss Starnes?"

"No, thank you, Porter. I can manage." With a smile, she left him, climbing the stairs to her own chamber.

The room was on the same floor as Adele's, but it faced the street instead of her aunt's small, formal garden. She was sometimes awakened by peddlers early in the morning, but she never minded. Clarissa preferred the street side of the house to the quieter side. Today, she was more thankful than ever that her window overlooked the street as she pulled a chair close to the window and waited.

Whoever went into a house had to come out sometime, and she wanted to get another glimpse of the most handsome man in the world — in her world, at least.

"I'd give a monkey to know why Cravenwell is footing the bill for our visit," whispered Max, his blue eyes taking in the lush surroundings in the small drawing room where the butler had left them to cool their heels until the master would see them.

"He has known Papa for ages," said Montgomery.

"Exactly," murmured Tristram. "And they have been feuding as long as they have known each other."

"His lordship will see you now."

The three men jumped up to follow the butler into the hall and up the wide stairs to the first floor and then on to the second. With a quick rap on a carved door, the butler opened it and motioned the visitors forward.

Though one wall had several windows, the chamber was dark. The windows were covered by velvet curtains in a deep blood red. The bed, too, was concealed by curtains in the same color. The brothers waited a moment for their eyes to adjust to the gloom.

"The Honorable Messieurs Darby, my lord," said the butler, bowing deeply and withdrawing from the room. He closed the door, shutting off more of the light.

"Well, don't just stand there like country loobies. Come over here and let me have a look at you. Met you once years ago, but you have grown up since then."

Obediently, the men stepped closer to the bed, their eyes widening as they took in the sight of the naked marquess lying prone, his mid-section covered by the sheet.

"How do you do?" Montgomery managed for them all.

"I do very well," said the old man with a cackle. "Move out of the way, girl." The scantily clad female, who had been massaging his shoulders, scrambled to the far side of the bed, and the marquess rolled over on his back and propped himself up on the pillows.

"Get those chairs over there and come here," he said. "And you needn't bother trying to avoid looking at Poppy. She's accustomed to men, ah, admiring her, aren't you?" A bony arm snaked out and pulled the girl to his side, into the candlelight.

As his brothers dragged three chairs closer to the bed, Montgomery said formally, "We would be happy to wait downstairs, my lord. When you are ready to . . ."

"I'm ready now," snapped the old man. "Go and pull back those demmed curtains so I can see what I've gotten myself into."

Montgomery stiffened and didn't move. Tristram rose and pulled back the window

26

curtains, the action sending light spilling across the bed and its two occupants. The girl pulled the sheet closer, but the old man twitched it away angrily.

"If I wanted to be covered, I would do it myself. Now sit down, gentlemen, while we conduct our business."

Tristram pulled on Montgomery's sleeve until he was seated, too. The marquess leaned forward, studying them in silence for a moment before expelling another of those grating cackles.

"Your father doesn't lie, at least. Yes, I see that you will do very well. The ladies will love them all, won't they, Poppy?"

"Yes, m'lord," came the small voice in reply.

"Yes, you'll do very well."

"Are we to, uh, stay here with you, my lord?" asked Tristram.

"With . . . Devil take you, boy. Why would I wish to saddle myself with three country bumpkins like you? No, I have rented a suite of rooms for you on St. James Street. You'll have one servant among the three of you, and a woman to clean for you. You've a line of credit at the bank — not limitless, but enough to allow each of you to give a creditable presentation. You'll be allowed full access to my stables. I never ride anymore, but I've still got several hacks from when I did. There's even a curricle or two."

"Thank you, sir," commented Max, his eyes growing wide in anticipation.

"Humph," grunted the marquess, studying them again. Reaching for a leather purse on the bedside table, the old man heaved it at Montgomery. "That should get you started. Barton, your servant, can fill you in on all the rest."

"I beg your pardon, my lord, but why are you doing this?" asked Montgomery.

"Your father did not explain my reasons to you, did he?"

"No, he did not."

"Good for him. At least he can keep his mouth shut better than he plays cards."

"So you are not going to tell us either?" asked Tristram.

"No, you needn't know the whys and wherefores. Just enjoy yourselves and get the business done. Oh, and one more thing. I have secured vouchers to Almack's for you. That will be your first appearance, Wednesday next, so be sure you have suitable clothes. They still wear knee breeches there. Attending Almack's is the only introduction to the *ton* you'll need. Once the ladies catch sight of you . . . that's all. Now go away. I've a mind to put Poppy here through her paces again."

The Darby brothers moved quickly toward the door and had almost made good their escape when the marquess halted them with a final word.

"Do remember, gentlemen, you are here to find wealthy wives. Do not spoil your chances by admitting to anyone that you are nothing but penniless country rustics."

Max took a step toward the bed, but Montgomery pulled him out the door.

"Come on," hissed Montgomery, shutting the door behind them. In a normal voice, he added, "Unless you want to get more of an eyeful than we already have."

"I wouldn't mind that," said Tristram, grinning at his older brothers and strolling down the hall to the stairs. "Something told me that coming to London was an educational experience not to be missed."

Clarissa saw the door open and eagerly leaned forward to catch the first glimpse of the handsome man who had entered the house not half an hour earlier. She grimaced as the blond boy exited first. Fidgeting with anticipation, she sank back as the next one left — dark and handsome, to be sure, but without that certain something which the third man possessed. There! There he was! Her eyes drank him in. She held her breath, fearing it would fog the windowpane.

He had to be all of six feet tall, with thick, wavy hair and a strong chin and nose. His brow crinkled as he gazed up at the sky, drinking in the sunshine. He clapped the other dark-haired one on the back, said something, and they all laughed. Clarissa's heart jumped up and turned over. She threw open the window, oblivious to the danger of being discovered. Their laughter drifted up to her, and she smiled, too.

Then they climbed into the waiting hackney and were gone. The sun disappeared behind a cloud, matching the light of the sky with her mood.

She knew how foolish she was being. But never before had the mere sight of a man made her weak in the knees. She had seen any number of handsome men — they flocked around Adele like bees to the honey pot, but this man had something in his face that . . . Oh, she was being foolish beyond permission. She would probably never see the man again. And if she did, Adele would be there, and then *he* would never notice Clarissa at all.

Hearing the front door open, Clarissa drew back, standing to one side to watch her beautiful cousin descend to the pavement with a man on each arm and several more clustering around her. Adele's pink parasol popped open, and they strolled toward the park. Clarissa shook her head. A pink parasol and a yellow gown — Bates was right. Adele had absolutely no sense of fashion.

She closed the window. Somehow, the thought failed to cheer her. Clarissa wandered toward the dressing table and stared at her image in the glass. Her copper-colored gown was fashionable and fitted her petite figure perfectly. She rather liked her dark brown hair, and her nose was decent, she thought, objectively. But the eyes were too dull to be thought pretty. And her mouth? Much too wide, she knew. The image of Adele's rosebud mouth came to mind, and Clarissa stuck out her tongue at her reflection. With a sigh, she drifted to the bed and threw out her arms, flopping across the bed in the most unladylike fashion.

Ten years since her parents had died. Ten years of being the poor relation. Never had she resented it. Never had she envied her cousin for her possessions — neither the beaux nor the gowns. But now, she would give anything to possess just one-tenth of Adele's beauty and charm, and all to attract a stranger whose kindly, handsome face made her heart turn flips.

Life was really quite cruel.

Two

"Trust me, Mr. Darby. Sharp's every bit as good a tailor as Weston, but he doesn't have the reputation yet, so his prices are much more reasonable."

"Hope you are right about this one, Barton," said Max, tapping their servant's shoulder and pointing to his booted feet. "You said Vickers was every bit as good a bootmaker as Hoby, and I can tell you, he ain't."

"So you have already said, Master Maxwell. I apologize for that. You must admit, however, that his *shoes* are quite acceptable."

"And so are the boots, Barton," commented Tristram. "Max has too high expectations of his boots and his horses. There are other things in this world . . . of . . . greater . . . import. I'll rejoin you in a few minutes," said Tristram, turning on his heel and walking to follow the pieman who was flying along the street shouting out his list of wares.

"I hope that boy buys a fruit pie. They do say the origin of the meat in those pies is questionable," said Barton, opening the door to the tailor's shop for his young masters to enter.

"Meaning what?" asked Max.

"Some say they make those pies out of cats or dogs."

"That's horrible," said Max with a shudder of his broad shoulders.

"Good afternoon, gentlemen. Mr. Barton told me you would be calling," said Sharp, the obsequious tailor.

"This is the Honorable Mr. Montgomery Darby, and this is his brother, the Honorable Mr. Maxwell Darby," announced Barton.

"Delighted to meet you, gentlemen. I thought there were to be three of you."

"There are. Our younger brother will be here shortly."

"Very good. Then perhaps we should begin with the measurements," said the tailor, pulling out a ribbon with the inches marked all along it. "My, my, Mr. Darby. I vow you gentlemen will be the making of me. I promise you. You will be the best advertisement a tailor could hope for, with these broad shoulders. So well-proportioned," he added, with a sigh.

"Then you'll see to it the gentlemen are rewarded?"

"Of course, Mr. Barton. It will be exactly as we agreed."

"What does that mean, Barton?" asked Montgomery.

"Simply put, for giving each of you a complete wardrobe at an excellent price, wardrobes which will be remarked upon by your new acquaintances, Mr. Sharp expects you to tell people, when they ask, that he is your tailor of choice."

"Well, I suppose we can do that."

"Excellent, gentlemen. Shall we look at the cloth?"

Two hours later, exhausted by the fatigue of choosing so many coats and other articles of clothing which Barton deemed requisite for a gentleman on the town, the three brothers made their way to the coffeehouse near their lodgings for supper. They had been up since early morning, a habit they had yet to break since arriving in London, much to their new servant's dismay. The sounds of the city were foreign to them, waking them earlier than usual and keeping them awake into the night. Barton speculated that soon, they would be arriving home at the hour they were now awakening. Furthermore, he cautioned them, they would need to accustom themselves to dining at eight o'clock or later, but now they were too hungry to wait.

Over their port, Montgomery said, "I know this Sharp fellow is giving us a very good price on our new clothes, but we still spent a fortune — more than I ever thought to spend on my wardrobe in the whole of my life."

"Relax, Montgomery. We're in London now. Things are more expensive," said Max.

"And we are more extravagant!" said Montgomery. "I mean, does a fellow really need so many coats? Only think of it, Max. You could have purchased that commission in the army that you always wanted with the amount we spent today."

"You know Papa promised Mama that none of her sons would ever be soldiers, so there is no need to belabor that point," said Max. Leaning closer, he added, "Besides, we need the clothes if we want to impress the ladies. Aren't you looking forward to cutting a bit of a dash, Montgomery? I mean, you might end up returning to Darwood Hall and never leaving it again. Don't you want to enjoy your stay in London?"

Montgomery grinned at his twin and nodded. "You are right. Besides, what is done is done, and I shall simply have to accept it. I do worry, however, about what we will do when the money runs out."

Tristram closed his sketchbook and looked at both of them, leaning forward and motioning to them to do the same.

"I thought the same thing," he whispered, "but Barton tells me we've only expended a small portion of the account set up by the marquess."

"A small portion? After this afternoon's work?" said Montgomery.

"Indeed. He said the marquess is very generous, and instructed him to make certain we had everything we needed. I think the old man is as queer as Dick's hatband."

"Perhaps, but I can't help but wonder . . ."

"No more wondering, Montgomery. Simply enjoy. Remember? Now, let's order another bottle of this ripping port. We'll take it back to our rooms and get roaring drunk."

"Really, Max, can't you think of anything besides pleasure?" said Montgomery.

"Not tonight." Max grabbed his brother's hand and pulled him to his feet. "What about you, little brother?"

"Oh, I think I'll sit here with my sketchbook a while longer. I'll join you later," said Tristram, waving them away.

When the twins were gone, he began to draw again, looking up impatiently when the landlord's large figure cast his work into shadow.

" 'Ere now, young gentleman. Wot you got there?"

"Just a quick sketch," he replied, politely. Showing the landlord the drawing, he added, "I hope you don't mind."

"Well, look at that. It's me! Wait a minute. Let me get the missus. Mrs. Turnbull, come 'ere. Quick!"

The rotund landlady bounded out of the kitchen, her face red with exertion and heat. "What's wrong, Mr. Turnbull?"

"Nothing's wrong! I wanted you to look at this. Who do you think that is?" he demanded, thrusting the sketch under his wife's nose.

"Why, I never! It's you! I've never seen such a good likeness. It could just open its mouth and speak, and I wouldn't know the difference."

"You're very kind," said Tristram, gently prying the book from her hands.

"I'll tell you wot, young gentleman. I'll give you another glass of ale if you'll let me have it."

"A drawing for a glass of ale?" said his

wife, shocked at such generosity.

"I've a mind to put it up on the wall, behind the counter. It won't half cause a stir when people sees it," said the landlord.

"I suppose I could do that, but you must allow me to give it to you as a gift, Mr. Turnbull," said Tristram.

"Naw, I couldn't."

"It would be my way of repaying you for allowing me to sit here from time to time, quietly working. I know the space here is valuable, and I worry about occupying the table when others might. . . ."

"You say no more, Mr., uh . . ."

"Darby, sir. Tristram Darby."

"I would consider it an honor, Mr. Darby, to have you sit here, sketching whatever you like to sketch."

"Thank you, Mr. Turnbull. And perhaps your good wife would allow me to draw her sometime?"

The middle-aged woman preened, blushing to the roots of her hair. "Oh, that would be wonderful, Mr. Darby. Just wonderful."

"Perhaps tomorrow morning, before . . . before you get so busy," said the tactful Tristram, rising and delivering a slight bow.

"Oh," she breathed. "I'll be here, Mr. Darby."

"Then I'll bid you good evening, Mr. and Mrs. Turnbull."

She dropped into a creditable curtsy, and the landlord lowered his gaze and gave a subservient nod. Whistling, Tristram made his way out of the coffeehouse and across the street.

Max and Montgomery were in the middle of a game of piquet. Barton sat close by, his hands busily mending the tear in Max's best coat. Until their clothes were delivered, their old things had to do.

"Where have you been, brat?" asked Max.

"Nowhere. I was wondering, Barton, if one wanted to go to Vauxhall Gardens, how does one get there?"

"You can go by carriage or by water, but you mustn't be considering that, Master Tristram, not until you have your clothes."

"It will be dark. Surely clothing will not make any difference. I want to see the famous waterfall."

"It's not really a waterfall, sir. It just looks like one. But back to the original problem. It might be dark, but the pathways are all lit, and people would see you, and you really do not want that to happen yet, Master Tristram."

"Wait until we have something to wear,

Tristram," said Montgomery. "Sharp has promised us each an ensemble or two by next Monday. We could go to the pleasure gardens then, if you like."

"Oh, very well. Only I don't enjoy cooling my heels like this."

"Take heart, halfling," said Max. "Tomorrow is Saturday. And then Sunday, we can go to services at St. . . ."

"Not at St. Paul's!" said the servant before covering his mouth at his own temerity. "I beg pardon, gentlemen. I only meant . . ."

"That we shouldn't show ourselves where Society can get a good look at us until we have the suitable clothes," said Montgomery, glaring at the servant and then at his brothers. "I begin to think all this was not such a good idea. If one must put on airs just to be thought suitable company, then I take leave to doubt the wisdom of our visit to London at all."

"Please, Mr. Darby, forgive me. I spoke in haste. If you decide to leave because of something I said, the marquess . . . That is, please reconsider, sir," said Barton, the color draining from his face.

"Don't worry, Barton," said Max. "Monty, here, gets too caught up in morals and principles. We're not going anywhere until we've had a taste of London. Shame on you, Monty, scaring poor Barton like that. If we leave, then what is to become of him, eh?"

"I suppose you're right, Max. All right, we will stay secluded until we can present a proper appearance."

"Besides, Mr. Darby, there's a nice little church just around the corner here. Probably much more what you're used to back home," said Barton.

"Good. That should do nicely."

"Thank you, sir. I'll just pop around tomorrow and find out what time services are."

When the servant had left them alone, the brothers' conversation turned immediately to Barton's transformation when he had thought they might leave London.

"Can't blame him," said Montgomery. "He would be out of a job without us."

"One would think so," said Tristram. "I wonder, though. It was more like he was afraid of what the marquess would do to him."

"You think the marquess might be blackmailing him or threatening him in some way?" said Max, always ripe for an adventure.

"You may have something, Max. It was

his mention of the marquess that made him lose his color," said Montgomery.

With a shiver, Tristram said, "I wouldn't put it past that old man. What do you think is the real reason he is helping us?"

"I would guess he owes Papa something — money, perhaps, but that would mean Papa had won at the tables," said Max.

"And we know that isn't very likely," said Tristram. "It makes no sense to me."

"Nor to me, but Barton is clearly frightened of the old man," said Max.

"But would a peer of the realm stoop to blackmail?" said Tristram.

"I wouldn't put anything past Cravenwell," said Montgomery.

"Sure you don't want to come along, Tris?" asked Max, early Monday morning.

Tristram's answer was a pillow thrown at his brother's head.

"I think we can take that as a 'no,' " said Montgomery, settling his hat on his head and putting on his leather gloves before following Max outside. "I hope the marquess left word with his grooms that we are to have access to his stables."

"He did. I went over to the mews the first day we were in London, when you and Tris were getting settled. They were very forthcoming. You're going to be impressed by the quality of the horseflesh, though why the marquess keeps so many . . . must cost him a fortune, here in the middle of London. I tell you, Monty, I wouldn't mind being able to afford such a stable."

"Control yourself, Max," said his pedantic twin. "We have yet to see a single lady, unless you count the few we have passed in the streets on the way to the bootmaker's, the tailor's, or the haberdashery."

"You can't blame a fellow for dreaming. And you can't tell me you haven't had the same dreams."

Montgomery shook his head and smiled. "Not me. I don't give a rap about horses. You know that."

"Not horses. I'm talking about row upon row of crops, each plant bending to the ground with its harvest. About fences mended properly and even a house without woodworm. You can't tell me you haven't dared to dream about all that since we started this little adventure," said Maxwell.

"All right. I do admit it. When have I not had that dream? But I am not foolish enough to think that one simple dowry is going to remedy all the ills at Darwood

Hall — especially when I haven't met a single young lady."

Maxwell chuckled and clapped his brother's back. "Don't worry, Monty. We'll meet them, and then we'll win them. I can feel it in my bones."

Montgomery replied with another deep chuckle and shook his head. "Now where have I heard those words before? Is that your voice I hear, Papa? Oh, sorry, I meant to say, Max."

"Very funny," replied his twin. "Ah, here we are. Down this alley, third gate."

Unlike many of London's fashionables, the Marquess of Cravenwell did not rent space for his horses. Instead, he owned the land where his cattle were stabled and his carriages were housed. This extravagance, especially for a man who no longer rode on horseback or drove his own carriage, was often remarked upon by the *ton*. The marquess, however, paid no heed to anyone's opinion other than his own.

"I told you it was bang up to the mark," said Max as he hailed one of the grooms.

"Good afternoon, Mr. Darby. And this must be one o' yer brothers. I'm Needham, the head groom. As 'is lordship says, if you need summat, you need Needham." The groom gave a hearty laugh and swung the gate wide. "Anytime you need a horse brought round t' your lodgings, all you have to do is send us a message."

"Thank you, Needham. I wanted my brother to see the stables, if you don't mind."

"Mind? Course not, sir. Th' Darby brothers are welcome 'ere anytime. Where's the other young gentleman?"

"Our brother Tristram doesn't often ride . . . or drive. Though, of course, he may require a carriage and driver from time to time."

"I see," said the groom, his frown showing that he didn't see at all.

"Our younger brother is of a bookish nature," said Maxwell.

"Oh, one of those. Well, he need only send for a carriage, and we'll be happy to oblige. I have a neat little barouche that would do fine for him. Now this horse, Mr. Darby, is the one your brother, Mr. Maxwell, thought you might like. She's a spirited sort, but not too showy."

"Thank you, Needham. I think she will do very well. What about you, Max?"

"Nothing but the best for me. Come over here," said Max, leading the way down the row of stalls. "This is Thunderlight, winner at Newmarket two years in a row."

"Trust you to choose the best of the stable, Max," said Montgomery. "Shall we put them through their paces?"

"I can't wait," said Max, who was already reaching for the bridle.

Ten minutes later, they were mounted and waiting for the groom to let them out of the gate.

"Just keep to the right when you get to the road. Then left when you see the big house with the black door. You'll find yourselves at Green Park in no time."

"Thank you, Needham," said Montgomery, following his brother, who was already halfway down the alley.

Montgomery allowed his mind to drift as his horse followed obediently behind Thunderlight. When on horseback, he always allowed Max to lead the way. It was easier that way. Since they were boys, Max had always been the headstrong one, especially when they were on horseback. It was as if Max became one with his horse, and nobody could stop them.

It was different when it came to dealing with people. Max's impetuous nature left people feeling bowled over and resentful, whereas Montgomery solved every dispute through diplomacy. Perhaps that was why he had settled into thinking of Mrs. Richland as a possible mistress for Darwood Hall. There didn't seem to be any reason for her not be its next mistress. Of course, that was before he had seen the golden-haired beauty framed in the window of the house next door to the Marquess of Cravenwell's town house. He shook his head. He would probably not encounter her again.

"Montgomery, this way," shouted Max, twisting in his saddle and giving his brother an impatient wave.

Montgomery dragged the reins around, and Parsnip, as he had learned his horse was called, obliged him by turning down the street that led to Green Park.

"I'm sorry, Max. I was woolgathering."

"Precisely why you will never be considered a dab hand with the horses. What has you so preoccupied?"

"Nothing. Just thinking about why we are here."

"Ah, thinking about the girl with the golden hair!"

"I was not. That is, I was, but I was telling myself we would probably never even meet, so that is not the same thing."

"I don't know. There cannot be that many parties to attend. The two of you are bound to cross paths sometime. And what about this Almack's? If the girl is anybody, according to Barton, she'll attend Almack's. So you see, big brother, you may very well meet this beauty again. All the more reason to pay attention when you're out in public. I mean, if she were looking out some other window and saw you, just then, practically falling off your mount from daydreaming . . . well, let us say, she would not be very impressed."

"Now you really are weaving a tale, Max. Nevertheless, I shall try not to disgrace myself, or you, for that matter. And do remember to follow Barton's advice and avoid any fashionables we might meet this morning. When our new riding gear has arrived . . ."

"Of course, but we will not meet anybody. Too early for the London fribbles, don't you know," said Max, acting very much the man about town.

"Nevertheless . . . what's that?" said Montgomery, pulling back on the reins and cocking his head to one side as the morning quiet was broken by the sound of drumming hooves.

"Sounds like a runaway horse," said Max, tensing in his saddle, ready to spring into action.

Just then, a small mare broke free from

the trees, the thundering hooves gradually slowing as its rider brought it under control.

"Now that's a beauty," said Max, grinning at his brother. Lifting the reins, he sent his horse trotting along the path to meet the mare and its rider. A round, dappled gray gelding carrying a round, gray-haired groom caught up with his mistress on the mare at the same time.

"Miss, I told you we couldn't keep up," said the groom, maneuvering his mount between Max and his mistress.

"I'm sorry, Mitch. I didn't mean to frighten you," said the dark-haired girl, all the while smiling as she peered around her groom at Max.

Max inched Thunderlight to one side and then back, catching her attention. "When I first heard your mare's hooves, I was afraid she was a runaway, but I can see, miss, that you had complete control over her."

"It was good of you to be concerned, sir," said the girl, her hazel eyes growing wide. "Why, you're . . . that is, you must be new to town."

Clarissa shooed her groom away, and he begrudgingly obeyed. She watched in growing excitement as the gentleman laughed and turned to motion his brother forward.

"Yes," he said, returning his attention to her. "We are just up from the country. Maxwell Darby, at your service, miss. And this is my brother, the Honorable Montgomery Darby. And you are?"

"My name is Clarissa Starnes. I am delighted to meet both of you," breathed Clarissa, wondering how in the world she could speak when her breath had been taken away. "As it happens, I saw your arrival in town. My aunt and uncle live next door to the Marquess of Cravenwell."

The one who had stolen her breath away leaned forward and said eagerly, "Then you must know who the golden-haired beauty in the window was that day."

Clarissa managed to keep the smile on her face, but her heart sank low. "That was my cousin, Adele Landis."

"Do you think you could present me to her? Perhaps on Wednesday at Almack's?" he asked, never knowing that he was tearing her heart apart.

"It would be my pleasure. Now, I really must go, gentlemen. My aunt allows me to ride in the park like this only when it is early, and no one is likely to be about, and

I see more people are arriving. Good day, gentlemen."

"Good day, Miss Starnes," said Max. When she had ridden a few paces, he added, "Did you see the lines on that mare, Monty? What a beauty! Perfect confirmation!"

Clarissa kicked her heels, and her mare sped away before she let loose the howl that was building in her breast. Not only did the man of her dreams prefer her cousin, but his brother looked at her and saw only her horse.

Things could not get much worse!

Clarissa hurriedly donned a round gown in soft yellow crepe, tying the sash with fumbling fingers. She was rarely summoned to her Aunt Frances's sitting room, so today had to be something special. Perhaps Adele had finally settled on a suitor.

Clarissa had arrived home to find too many servants cleaning the front hall and sitting room. Questioning Porter, she had found out that Lord Benchley had come to call and was even then closeted with Mr. Landis.

Clarissa smiled and started up the stairs when he added, "Your aunt has requested that you join her in her sitting room."

Clarissa stopped outside the closed door and took a deep breath, smoothing her gown. After a soft knock, her aunt's maid opened the door and stood to one side to allow her to enter.

Clarissa's brows went up when she realized Adele was seated beside her mother, who was looking quite miserable. She had supposed Adele would have been summoned to the study to receive Lord Benchley's offer. Nearby, Miss Anderson sat with her knitting, the needles softly clicking in the silence.

Dipping a quick curtsy, Clarissa took the chair her aunt indicated. "Good morning, Aunt. How are you today?"

Heaving a sigh, Frances Landis patted her still-golden hair and said, "I am fine, dear girl. A bit disappointed, perhaps, but I am fine."

"Mama, I cannot help it if I do not wish to accept Lord Benchley's offer. I need more time," said Adele.

The door was thrown open as her cousin uttered this last, and Clarence Landis strode into the room as the door slammed shut behind him. With a scowl, he sent the maid scurrying into the dressing room.

"What the devil is wrong with this one, Miss Maggoty?" he demanded, standing in front of his daughter, his legs spread and his arms crossed.

"Mr. Landis, surely there is no need for . . ."

"Not now, madam. I am speaking to our headstrong, scapegrace of a daughter!" he roared.

A single tear trickled down Adele's cheek. "I am so sorry to disappoint you, Papa. You know that."

"Well, you . . . I . . . oh, blast!" he said, sitting down in the spindly chair by his daughter's side and taking her hand. "My dearest child, you know I only wish for you to be happy. And Lord Benchley . . . The man has wealth, title, and no need of an heir since he has two sons already."

"He is a bit old," ventured the timid Mrs. Landis.

Bristling, her husband snapped, "He is five years younger than I am."

His daughter soothed his wounded sensibilities by saying, "Yes, Papa, and in a father, that is quite young, but as a husband for me . . ."

"I know," he grumbled. "But Lord Benchley would be good to you, Adele. He would never make unreasonable demands. He would spoil you almost as much as I do."

"And I am not saying no, Papa. I am not well acquainted with Lord Benchley. I want to get to know him better, to see if I can like him."

"Very well, you will get the chance on Thursday. We are to attend the theater as his guests — all of us," he said, rising and then bending over to kiss the top of his daughter's head.

Then he was gone, and the ladies breathed sighs of relief.

"If you will excuse me, girls, I must lie down," said Clarissa's aunt, rising and trailing out of the sitting room.

"If you should need me, girls, I will be in my room," said Miss Anderson.

When they were alone, Adele wriggled in her seat and smiled smugly. "Not a bad situation. I can still enjoy the entire Season, but I already have a very suitable offer to consider."

"Adele, do you mean you plan to accept Lord Benchley?" asked Clarissa. "If so, you should simply do so."

"Oh, but I might lose all my suitors, and I am not willing to give them up yet. Besides, what do you care? Have you developed a *tendre* for the ancient earl?"

"He is hardly ancient, and no, I have not developed a *tendre* for him," said Clarissa, keeping her tone even and indifferent. If Adele suspected she had an interest in Lord Benchley, she would forever torture her with teasing. She did not, of course, and her thoughts drifted back to the handsome Mr. Darby. Thank heavens Adele had not been present to see her reaction to him!

"Do not drag it out too long," she advised her fickle cousin. "Men do not appreciate having to wait."

"Oh, and you are such an expert on men, I suppose," said Adele, rising and floating out of the room.

"No," whispered Clarissa when her cousin had gone. "I am not an expert, but I am considerate, something you have never been."

After several moments, she followed her cousin from the room, going down the stairs to her uncle's study to select a book from the well-stocked shelves. She selected a well-worn volume and settled on the small leather sofa, tucking her feet under her gown.

It was a book she had read many times, from cover to cover — a surprising choice for a young lady, perhaps, but it set her to daydreaming more quickly than any novel of the day.

She was lost in the description of a grand castle when her uncle's voice caused her to jump.

"Didn't mean to startle you, Clarissa." Looking over her shoulder, he commented, "Reading your travel book again, puss?"

She smiled and closed it, straightening up so that he might join her on the sofa.

"Wish I could find something that would take me away as easily as that."

"Adele will settle on a husband soon, Uncle. I feel certain of it."

"I hope you may be right, my dear. And when she does, then we shall see what we can do for you, eh? Although, truth be told, your aunt and I will miss you terribly."

"How sweet of you to say so," said Clarissa, smiling up at him. "And I am in no hurry to leave, Uncle."

"Well, that's a comfort, then. I worry, sometimes, that I have not done right by you. I hate to think what Hetty would say."

"Not done right?" she said. "You took me in and have treated me like a daughter all these years! I count myself very blessed."

"You're a good girl, Clarissa," he said,

picking up the book beside him and opening it.

After a moment, Clarissa returned to her own book and dreams.

Three

"The hallowed portals of Almack's," quipped Tristram as the Darby brothers stood on the pavement looking up at the unimpressive façade of the famous assembly hall.

"Yes, and we are not going to meet anyone if we continue to stand on the pavement," said Max. "Let's get this over with."

"Spoken like a man eager to saddle himself with a wife," whispered Tristram, following on Max's heels.

"Tristram, try to remember why we are here and behave yourself," said Montgomery. "And pray do not pull out that small notebook I know you have hidden in your coat and start doodling."

"Your wish is my command," said the young man, executing a perfect bow.

"I just wish we didn't have to wear these blasted knee breeches," said Max.

"Just look around you. All the gentlemen are wearing them," said Montgomery as they climbed the steps and entered the assembly hall.

"I know, I know," he grumbled. "At least our coats are well-cut. That tailor really does know what he's doing."

"Yes, but I should have had the dark blue instead of the black. The blue would have suited my coloring much better," complained Tristram, surprising both his brothers who stopped and stared at him. He ducked his head and said gruffly, "What are you staring at? Can't a fellow want to look his best?"

"Certainly, we just didn't realize you would be the one who would turn into a dandy," said Maxwell, cuffing his brother on the arm.

Ignoring his brothers, Montgomery's thoughts turned immediately to searching the room for the blonde beauty — Miss Landis. He quickly spied her cousin who was standing at the edge of a group of young men. She brightened when she saw him and gave a timid little wave. He nodded in return, but quickly lost interest in the cousin as Miss Landis emerged from the center of that group of gentlemen, her dimples dimpling and her eyes shining as she took the arm of some lucky devil and allowed him to lead her onto the floor.

"Good evening. The Messieurs Darby,

n'est-ce pas?" said a matron of some thirty years.

"That is correct," said Montgomery, dragging his attention away from the light of his life. "I am Montgomery Darby, this is my brother Maxwell Darby, and this is Tristram Darby."

"Cravenwell told me you would be here this evening, and I knew, when I saw three handsome strangers, it must be you. I am Lady Cowper. I am the one who sent you your vouchers."

"You are too kind, my lady," said Montgomery, fully cognizant of the great service she had done for them since Barton had told him over and over.

"Think nothing of it. You must tell me if I can do anything else for you while you are in London. Right now, I would like to introduce each of you all to a charming young lady."

"Again, you are too kind, my lady," said Montgomery, offering her his arm while his two brothers followed after them.

They stopped in front of a rather plain young lady who was dressed in flounces from just under the bustline to the floor. Each time she moved, she sent them fluttering.

"Miss Davis, allow me to present to you

a charming young man who has asked if he might have the next dance. This is Mr. Darby, Mr. Tristram Darby."

"How do you do, Miss Davis," said Tristram, obediently stepping forward and bowing. This action met with a titter and a curtsy that sent her dress into motion.

"You will look after him, won't you, Miss Davis? Mr. Darby is new to London," said Lady Cowper, causing the young lady to giggle again.

"It will be a pleasure, Mr. Darby."

"I knew I could count on you, Miss Davis. Come along, gentlemen," said Lady Cowper. "Ah, there is Lady Letitia — widowed last year when her husband was killed at Waterloo. Such a shame. Lady Letitia, how wonderful to see you again. And this is your sister, Miss Taylor, is it not?"

"Good evening, my lady," said the elder of the two girls.

"Ladies, allow me to present Mr. Montgomery Darby and Mr. Maxwell Darby. They are new to London, but we are fortunate they have finally found their way."

"Good evening," they all said, exchanging bows and curtsies.

Montgomery and Max quickly secured the ladies as their partners in the next dance which was just beginning. It was to be a waltz, and Max shot a look of panic at Montgomery, who nodded confidently and swept Lady Letitia onto the dance floor.

"Do we dare?" asked Max.

"I am sorry, Mr. Darby, but I have not yet received permission to waltz from the patronesses. I will understand completely if you wish to ask someone else," said Miss Taylor.

"No, no. To tell the truth, I have only just learned the waltz, and the fear of treading on your toes was making me exceedingly nervous," said Max, breathing a sigh of relief.

Miss Taylor giggled, a sweet, natural sound that had nothing to do with practiced flirtation, and Max felt his shoulders relax. This was no different from the assemblies at home where he always found the girls were pleased to see him.

"Perhaps you'll grant me the next dance," he said, turning the force of his blue eyes on her. "They tell me I am rather good at the quadrille."

"That would be wonderful," said Miss Taylor, smiling up at him. "Where are you from, Mr. Darby?"

"Cornwall. Our estate is near the coast."

"I had a friend at school who was from

Cornwall. Marion Peabody. Perhaps you are acquainted with her?"

"No, I'm afraid not. It is a very large area," said Max, feeling his confidence grow. He nodded toward Tristram as he swept past with Miss Davis in his arms. And then Montgomery passed by, too.

"I must admit," said Miss Taylor shyly, "that I am quite looking forward to dancing the waltz. It seems to be such an invigorating dance."

"Quite so. Of course, I have only practiced it a few times and then only with my brother."

She giggled again, and Max thought, that after a week in the unfamiliar territory that was London, he had finally found his niche — a place to be comfortable, basking in a pretty lady's admiration.

"Tell me, Miss Taylor, do you ride?"

Montgomery found the movements of the waltz extremely annoying. Here he was, trying his best to keep his eyes on Miss Landis, and instead, he was saddled with another female, who was so close, he could not very well ignore her. And he never knew where to look for his quarry as the irregular movements sent her flouncing all over the place.

To make matters worse, Lady Letitia was

a chatty little thing, constantly inserting silly questions that required his attention.

"Do you not think so?" she asked once more, making Montgomery wince.

He had no idea what she was talking about. Feeling like a gudgeon and giving a thoughtful nod, he said, "I suppose so."

"I knew you would agree with me. I mean, why shouldn't a young lady, especially a widow, be allowed to drive herself through the park in a curricle? My father is merely being dull."

"I feel certain your father has your best interests at heart, my lady," said Montgomery, feeling like a veritable cawker. What the devil was he thinking, giving a young female advice about how to go on in Society? He vowed to pay closer attention for the rest of the dance. Besides, he thought, looking down at the lady and really seeing her for the first time, she had lovely eyes.

Uncertain what topics she had already covered, Montgomery smiled and said, "Tell me more about yourself, Lady Letitia."

This was all the encouragement the talkative lady needed to launch into another long monologue. Montgomery, however, paid close attention to her conversation so that he replied appropriately when she asked him a question.

Finally, the music came to an end, and he took her arm and they promenaded around the room before he returned her to her sister. Free at last, Montgomery immediately sought out Miss Starnes to secure an introduction to her ravishing cousin.

Bowing low before Miss Starnes, his eyes betrayed where his interest lay as he gazed at her cousin.

"Good evening, Miss Starnes. So happy to see you have come to no harm from your outing yesterday."

"You are very kind," said Clarissa, pursing her lips in annoyance. She studiously avoided meeting his eyes, knowing that if she did, she would immediately comply with his silent request for an introduction to Adele.

After a moment of silence while he waited, she could put it off no longer.

"Mr. Darby, allow me to introduce you to some people. This is Mr. Pitchly, Lord Grant, and this is Mr. Sweet and Mr. Phelps," said Clarissa, pausing as everyone murmured polite "how do you do's." Finally, she said flatly, "And this is my cousin, Miss Landis."

Montgomery bowed deeply and said,

"Delighted to make your acquaintance, Miss Landis."

Adele smiled and gave a slight curtsy. "Clarissa mentioned having met you in the park. You are just arrived from the country, are you not?"

"Yes, my two brothers and I arrived last week."

"Only last week? But you look very elegant tonight, Mr. Montgomery. Weston?" asked the Incomparable.

"No, my man suggested a new tailor, a Mr. Sharp on New Bond Street," said Montgomery, just as Barton had instructed him. "Probably just a friend of my servant, but I am pleased with his work."

"Indeed," said Mr. Pitchly, raising his quizzing glass and magnifying his eye terribly as he stared at the coat. "I would have guessed Weston. Sharp, you say?"

"That's right," said Montgomery. "They are beginning the next set, Miss Landis. Dare I hope you will do me the honor?"

"I am sorry, Mr. Darby. I am promised to Lord Benchley."

Everyone stood back as an older man of some forty years arrived to claim his prize.

"Would you like to request the next dance?" Miss Landis prompted when Montgomery glared in silence.

"What? Oh, yes, might I have the . . ."

"Certainly, Mr. Darby. Perhaps you would care to partner poor Clarissa in this set."

"My pleasure," said Montgomery, offering his arm to Clarissa and leading her into the same square as Lord Benchley and Miss Landis.

The quadrille was familiar to Montgomery, so he had to pay little attention while performing the steps. This gave him more time to study Miss Landis, a pastime that was quickly becoming an obsession.

When he had come together with Miss Starnes for the fourth time and still made no effort at conversation, she took matters into her own hands.

"The least you can do, Mr. Darby, is to refrain from gazing at my cousin like a moon-sick calf. You are making a cake of yourself."

"I beg your pardon," he replied, shocked at her speech and its accompanying glare.

"You heard me," she hissed before they were parted by the dance once again.

Montgomery had himself well in hand by the time he met with Miss Starnes again. Very much on his dignity, he kept his eyes on her alone and intoned, "Hasn't the weather been fine the past few days?"

Clarissa giggled, her hazel eyes coming to life. "Much better, Mr. Darby. Thank you."

"You are quite welcome, Miss Starnes. And tomorrow, do you think it might rain?"

"I believe it might," she replied, lifting her nose in the air before spoiling the effect with another throaty chuckle.

Montgomery grinned, his dark eyes dancing like midnight fires, and he quite forgot to gawk at Miss Landis for the remainder of the quadrille.

When it was over, Montgomery offered his arm to Miss Starnes and very properly escorted her back to Miss Anderson, the chaperone she shared with her cousin.

"Thank you for an eye-opening dance, Miss Starnes," he said with a wink.

"My pleasure, Mr. Darby. I hope I was not too blunt."

"Only as blunt as was necessary. You had every right to ring a peal over me. I was being quite rude, and though I am from the country, I assure you, my manners are usually much better. I apologize for neglecting you."

Miss Starnes blushed and dropped her eyes. In any other female, Montgomery would have considered the action flirtatious, but Miss Starnes was not that sort. She was more of a brick, a chum. When she looked up at him, he patted her hand resting on his arm.

"I say, Miss Starnes, you wouldn't happen to know what your cousin's favorite flower is?"

She hesitated — fishing for the correct answer, he guessed.

"Daisies," she said, smiling sweetly. "Daisies are Adele's favorite flower."

"Daisies," he murmured, his attention drawn to Miss Landis as she returned with Lord Benchley.

The musicians struck up a waltz, and Montgomery felt his heart skip a beat as he held out his arm for Miss Landis. With a simper, she took his arm and allowed him to lead her onto the floor. Though mindful of the requisite distance that needed to remain between them, Montgomery gave himself up to the complete bliss of holding her in his arms.

She wore a gown of pale blue that matched her eyes. Her eyes were wide as she gazed at him, a smile on her rosebud mouth.

Remembering Miss Starnes's lecture, Montgomery opened his mouth, then snapped it closed when no sound was emitted. His fatuous grin faded, and he swallowed twice before attempting speech again.

"Hasn't the weather been lovely the past few days?"

"Quite. I simply dote on sunshine."

"Then you must enjoy the country."

"The country? No, I much prefer town. Why, there is always something to do here. At home, I get moped to death in a matter of days."

"I . . . I see. I have not been in London very long, but I find there are times when I grow bored here. At home, I always have things to do on my estate."

"Ah, yes, your estate. I understand it has been in your family for hundreds of years," she said.

"Yes, there have been Darbys at Darwood Hall for over three hundred years."

"The estate must be very large by now," she said.

"Not so large," said Montgomery, searching for another topic. He could not tell her how little of the original land was left with the house. Not yet. When he had won her, then he would tell her.

"Do you have any brothers or sisters, Miss Landis?"

"No, I am an only child, my father's only heir."

"Really? I had no idea." That much was true. He hadn't bothered to ask anyone if Miss Landis was an heiress. Having seen her once, he knew he wanted her for his own. He hadn't even considered her fortune. It was just good luck that she would have one someday.

"And you, Mr. Darby. You have brothers, do you not?"

He smiled down at her. Evidently, she had been busy inquiring about him since waving at him from her window. Things were going very well.

"Yes, my twin brother, Maxwell, and my younger brother, Tristram. We are all visiting London together."

"And are they as handsome as you are?"

"You are too kind, Miss Landis."

"Only truthful. I think . . . Really, who is that boy who keeps popping out from behind that pole?" she demanded crossly.

"What boy?" asked Montgomery, his heart sinking as the "boy" appeared again. "I'll thrash him to within an inch of his life," he said through gritted teeth.

"I beg your pardon?"

"Nothing. Never mind, Miss Landis.

When this waltz is over, I will tend to the young rapscallion."

"How gallant of you, Mr. Darby."

The music ended, and Montgomery rushed Miss Landis back to her chaperone so he could take care of Tristram.

He was making his way across the emptying dance floor when two of the guests grabbed Tristram by the shoulders and hauled him out from his hiding spot. Montgomery quickened his steps.

"Really, gentlemen, I was only sketching some of the guests."

"We don't need your sort in here. We'll just see what the patronesses have to say about this," said one man, jerking Tristram's arm roughly.

Tristram threw off his captors and took the stance Max had taught him when facing a fight.

"I told you . . ."

"Tristram, what is going on?" Recognizing Mr. Pitchly, one of Miss Landis's admirers, Montgomery stiffened. "Is there a problem, Mr. Pitchly?"

"This young rascal has been annoying the ladies," said the very proper Mr. Pitchly.

"Really? Tristram, hand it over." Montgomery accepted the small notebook and flipped through it. Holding it open to one very flattering drawing of a young lady, he said, "Surely this young lady would not be annoyed with an admirer who simply wanted to capture her beauty."

The other man chuckled and commented, "Never seen Miss Criswell look better."

"That's true enough," said Pitchly with a sneer. "Very well, but this is not the place, young man. Next time, leave your notebook at home."

"And so I told him, but he does like to draw," said Montgomery, clasping Tristram around the shoulders before his sharp-witted brother could deliver one of his scathing rejoinders.

When they were alone, Tristram growled, "Conceited ape. And how dare you show them my drawings!"

"How dare you do what could get all of us thrown out of this place. I told you to behave, to keep our goal in mind, and what do you do? Cause a stir by popping out here and there, frightening the ladies."

"I warrant your lady wasn't frightened," muttered Tristram.

"What do you mean by that?" demanded Montgomery.

"Oh, nothing. Look, I am going to get

something to drink. You can go back to gazing at the blonde beauty. I promise I shall behave," he added.

Tristram put his hand out for his note-book, and Montgomery returned it to him reluctantly.

"Do not worry. I shan't draw anymore tonight." As Tristram pocketed the book, he added, "I hope you know what you're getting into, big brother."

"What do you mean by that?" asked Montgomery.

"Oh, nothing. Never mind. Go back to your lady."

Montgomery watched Tristram as he made his way to the refreshment tables without speaking to another person.

Looking across the crowded ballroom, Montgomery smiled. He was certain he was getting exactly what he wanted. With the light of determination in his eyes, he headed toward his quarry.

Before the evening was over, Montgomery secured another set with Miss Landis, and he watched her as she smiled and flirted with every other partner. He had no desire to ask another lady to dance. Unacquainted with the ways of the *ton,* it never occurred to him that other eyes were noticing his intense interest in the beautiful blonde, too.

When Miss Landis came off the dance floor after one more waltz, her cheeks a charming pink, Montgomery could not resist asking her for yet another dance. Cocking her head to one side, Miss Landis hesitated.

"Miss Adele, I must pro—" began her chaperone, Miss Anderson.

"Adele, surely you are not . . ." tried Miss Starnes.

Laying her hand on Montgomery's arm, Miss Landis smiled and said, "I cannot dance with you again, Mr. Darby, for it simply isn't done, but I would be quite content if you could discover some little bench where we might have a comfortable coze."

"I would be honored," he said, offering his arm and leading her away from her friends and chaperone. Montgomery frowned, unable to ignore the collective gasp that accompanied their departure.

When they were seated near the dance floor where they could watch the others, Montgomery asked, "Why were they trying to prevent you from accompanying me? Did I say or do something wrong?"

With a smug smile, Miss Landis shook her head. "No, they are just old-fashioned.

They are too afraid of Society and its little unspoken rules."

"I don't understand."

"Of course you do not, Mr. Darby. You are just up from the country, and that is all to the good. If anyone should dare to censure me for keeping company with you during this dance, I shall merely explain that, since you are from the country, you did not know about the outmoded rule about never sharing more than two dances with a man who is not one's husband, or at the very least, one's fiancé. And I will tell them that I simply didn't have the heart to tell you."

"But Miss Landis, this is terrible," said Montgomery, shocked to the core.

"Why, Mr. Darby? Do you not wish to spend this time with me?"

"Certainly I do, but I would never have asked if I had known it might endanger your reputation."

She giggled and batted her blue eyes at him, until he smiled again. "Never fear, Mr. Darby. You will not be questioned, though you may be teased a little. As for me, I shall manage to get through this. It is nothing, I assure you. Now, let us not speak of it anymore."

"If you wish," he said, groping for another thread of conversation and finding speech impossible. Seated beside her, he found his thoughts jumbled and far too warm for propriety.

"Only look at Lady Letitia's gown. Have you ever seen anything so dowdy?"

"Lady Letitia? I thought she looked quite charming," said Montgomery.

"But you cannot claim to know what is fashionable since you are new to London. I shall instruct you. Take that one, for instance. That is Lady Hurst. She is quite wealthy. Her husband sits in Parliament. Her gown is decidedly fashionable. Unfortunately, it is not at all suited to a woman of her age and size. And the color? Abominable!"

They sat in silence for a moment before Miss Landis opened her fan with a flip of her wrist and leaned closer, whispering, "The lady in the purple. Surely you will agree that her gown is impossibly hideous."

Montgomery looked at the lady in question and smiled. "It is rather unattractive," he agreed, feeling guilty for doing so, but enjoying the way Miss Landis smiled at him.

Closing the fan and giving her head a little shake, she gazed at the ceiling and asked, "Tell me, Mr. Darby, do you go to the theater tomorrow night?"

"I . . . I suppose so," said Montgomery. "We have not yet done so, and we want to see everything while we are here."

"Then you must come by Lord Benchley's box during the intermission."

"Lord Benchley's box?"

"Yes, you met him earlier. Lord Benchley is courting me, you see, and my family and I are to be his guests tomorrow night. So, if you wish to see me . . ."

Montgomery stiffened and said, "Benchley is courting you? Then am I to wish you happy?"

She gave a trill of laughter and rapped his arm with her fan in the most endearing manner. "Gudgeon. Just because a gentleman is courting me, it does not mean I have accepted him yet."

"But your father has agreed to the marriage?" He could not keep the overwhelming dejection out of his voice.

"Papa will not agree to anything until I say so, Mr. Darby, and I have not yet made my choice." Miss Landis studied him for a moment, brows raised, as if appraising his value, his attributes. "I must tell you, Mr. Darby, that my decision has become much more difficult since this evening began."

Montgomery's heart sang, but he managed a polite, "Is that so, Miss Landis?"

"Oh, quite so, but I'm afraid our time this evening has ended with the music. Even I would not dare to stay in your company for a fourth dance. Good evening, Mr. Darby," she said.

Montgomery scrambled to his feet as she rose. He bowed over her hand and then straightened to gaze into her eyes. "Until tomorrow night."

Miss Landis smiled and walked away, rejoining her cousin and her chaperone. Montgomery glanced around the hall and spied Max and Tristram. A simple signal, and they nodded, heading for the doors. If he could neither dance nor be in company with Miss Landis again, there was no reason to remain at Almack's.

One last, lingering look at her astonishing beauty, and Montgomery left the ballroom.

Since Almack's was only a short stroll from their lodgings on St. James Street, the brothers had elected to walk home. They were quiet as they strolled, each lost in his own thoughts. Upon entering their small sitting room, they were accosted by Barton, who leapt to his feet, wiped the sleep from his eyes, and set about removing coats and plying them with questions.

"And you, Master Tristram. Did you dance with any young ladies?"

"A few," he replied.

"Mostly, he just hid behind pillars and frightened them with his stares," said Montgomery.

"What?" demanded Max, who had been unaware of Tristram's near ejection from the hallowed hall.

"Oh dear," groaned Barton, pausing in his efforts to brush a spot from Montgomery's coat.

Montgomery frowned at the servant, but smiled when he saw the cause of the man's distress.

"Never fear, Barton, I'm certain you will be able to get that out. It is not a tragedy, after all — only a coat."

"One can only hope," said the man weakly.

"Forget the coat. Tell me what happened," said Max.

"Nothing happened. I became immersed in my drawing and failed to notice these two louts heading toward me."

"They were all for throwing him out," said Montgomery. "But I persuaded them that he was harmless by showing them a very flattering drawing of one of the young ladies present. Apparently, they decided he was only a want-wit and dropped the matter."

"It was nothing of the sort. I took my stand, just like you showed me, Max, and they were too terrified to tangle with me," said Tristram, flopping down on the closest chair and opening the offending notebook.

"I cannot leave you two alone for a minute," said Max, adopting a superior air. "What with Tris coming close to fisticuffs and you, Montgomery . . ."

"What the devil is that supposed to mean?" said his twin.

"It means, old fellow, that I had to go about putting out fires of speculation about you and Miss Landis."

"I fail to see why. I did nothing untoward."

"Now, now, no need to act high and mighty with me. I know you didn't know that you were not supposed to have three dances, but Miss Landis did. Everyone said so."

Montgomery grabbed his brother's cravat and gave him a shake. "I'll not have you saying anything against Miss Landis, Max."

Max backed away, his smile widening. "Hey, I am all for you winning Miss Landis — hand, foot, and . . . no, no, do not draw my cork, for I have no desire to retaliate. I was as surprised as you to discover that everyone was watching you. I mean, have these people nothing better to do than count the number of dances a fellow has with his lady love?"

"And how many did he have?" asked the stricken butler.

"What do you care, Barton?" snapped Montgomery, pushing the servant's hands away as he tried to remove his cravat.

His head sinking low, the servant said, "Nothing, sir, except that I did promise his lordship that I would look after you, and if you have landed in the briars due to my failure to educate you on the ways of Society . . . well, I cannot help but . . ."

"No need to be a regular jaw-me-dead, Barton," said Max. "I took care of it. Told everyone that in Cornwall, it was nothing to dance four or five times with the same chit. Made sure everyone was aware that m' brother was naught but a country bumpkin. Whoa!" he exclaimed, handily catching the pillow Montgomery threw at his head.

"Four or five times?"

"Devil a bit," said Tris. "Max, you are going to give poor Barton the apoplexy. Montgomery danced with Miss Landis only twice."

"Twice? Then that's all right," said the servant, clearing the chairs of the various coats and waistcoats, and toddling toward the bedrooms. "Will there be anything else this evening?"

"No, go to bed, Barton," said Montgomery. When the servant was gone, he turned to his twin and demanded, "What were they really saying?"

"Not much. It was more a question of the way their noses went up when you and Miss Landis sat on that bench for the third dance."

"Yes, she did warn me that it might cause talk. But what could I do? At that point, I could hardly abandon her."

"Nor did you want to, judging from the way you neglected every other female this evening in favor of watching Miss Landis. Really, Montgomery, even I know better than to wear my heart on my sleeve like that," said Tristram.

"I . . . I know. I just couldn't bring myself to ask anyone else once I had danced with her. It seemed pointless."

"So you think you have found your

bride," said Max, sitting down across from his twin and studying him intently.

"Yes, I . . . that is, I have found her, but I do not think much of my chances with her," he said miserably. "She invited me to visit her during the interval in a box to-morrow night at the theater."

"Well, there you go. It sounds to me as if she has already made her choice," said Max.

"You would not say that if you knew the whole. The box belongs to a Lord Benchley, who is practically in his dotage, who has asked for her hand in marriage. Her father is only waiting for her to make up her mind."

"But that's a good sign — I mean, if she is not leaping at his offer, then there is still hope for you."

"Humph! A man who can afford his own box at the theater or a man with a dwindling estate and a crumbling house," said Montgomery, running his hands through his dark hair.

Tristram rose and patted his eldest brother's shoulder. "Chin up. If she were not interested, Montgomery, she would not have put her reputation in danger in that manner."

Montgomery brightened and said,

"Thank you, Tristram. I had not thought of that. I'm just tired. I'm going to bed."

"Me, too," said Max, rising and following his twin out of the room.

Tristram dropped onto the chair his brother had just vacated and opened the small sketchbook again, flipping through the pages until coming to the last drawing. Miss Landis stared back at him, her rosebud-shaped mouth fixed in a twisted smile, her glance brittle and cold.

"As I said before, big brother, I only hope you know what you are getting into."

Four

Clarissa could not believe how tired, miserable, and angry she felt, and yet, still she rose early the next morning for a gallop in Green Park just as she had every morning that week. She admonished herself for her foolishness — hoping to encounter Mr. Darby was ridiculous. Even so, she put on her prettiest habit, tied back her long, straight hair, settled her most becoming bonnet on her head, and set forth at the preposterous hour of nine o'clock.

It was not as if she would not see him that evening. Adele had told her that he would be visiting Lord Benchley's box at the theater that evening. This, however, was not sufficient for Clarissa. She hoped beyond hope that Mr. Montgomery Darby might be out for an early, solitary ride, so that she might spend a few minutes alone with him. Her groom would be there, but he did not count. Perhaps, without Adele close by, Mr. Darby might notice how pretty her habit was and how well it suited her.

What was it about Mr. Darby that sent

her heart into palpitations? His twin brother was equally handsome, though she did think Montgomery's dark eyes were much more lively. It certainly wasn't his expertise on the dance floor. His waltzing had been merely adequate.

And while there was a certain kindness in his face, that did not explain the jolt of electricity she felt whenever he entered her sphere. There was some magic at work between them.

Clarissa turned her mare toward home. There had been no sign of either Darby brother. Perhaps she was merely fooling herself. Perhaps the magic was only one-sided. Mr. Darby certainly did not pay her any special heed when her cousin was in the vicinity.

Adele. There was another problem. If Adele decided she wanted Montgomery Darby, then she would have him. Everyone knew that he was quite wealthy. That information had been circulating around the *ton* since the brothers had arrived. Being the only child of a doting father, Adele's fortune would be immense one day. The size of her dowry was incredible. It would be a suitable match for them both.

To be fair, Adele was also regarded as a diamond of the first water.

Clarissa swished her riding crop against her mare's withers, and the mare jumped ahead as if shocked by this. Heaving a sigh, Clarissa stroked the glossy neck and apologized.

Perhaps she would plead the headache that evening. To see him fawning over Adele would prove very painful, and there was no need for her to go since Miss Anderson would be there. She loved the theater. No, there was no reason in the world for Clarissa to put herself through such pain.

But then she would not get to see Mr. Darby.

She would go, she decided. Seeing Mr. Darby would be worth the heartache.

"Oh, Snowdrop, why must I be such a fool?" she asked the little mare as she turned toward home.

When she entered the front hall, the butler pointed to a huge bouquet of greenery and spring daisies and said, "Miss Starnes, these flowers have arrived."

"How lovely," she said, smiling at the proper butler.

"They are for Miss Landis," said Porter.

"Of course they are," said Clarissa, having difficulty keeping her face straight. They had to be from Mr. Darby.

"But they make her sneeze, miss. She told me to throw them out, but as daisies are your favorites, I thought you might like to have them placed in your room."

"How thoughtful of you, Porter. Yes, thank you. That would be lovely."

When he turned to call a footman forward, Clarissa snatched the card off the table and put it in her pocket.

In her room, with Adele's bouquet of daisies, she opened the card. *From your ardent admirer. Mr. Darby.*

Clarissa tucked the note into her desk drawer.

"One of these days, Mr. Darby, I hope you will be saying that to me."

The rest of their wardrobes arrived Thursday afternoon. While the brothers were admiring their new clothes, they were shocked when Barton told them they needed to go back to Sharp's and have even more clothes made up. A gentleman of fashion, he proclaimed, might change his coat four times in one day, and what they possessed so far, while adequate, was not enough to proclaim them for what they were.

"And what are we, Barton? We have never claimed to be anything more than country gentry," said Montgomery.

"To be sure, sir, but you do wish to give the impression . . . What I mean to say is, you want everyone to know that you are men of means."

"But that's the point, Barton, we are not men of means," said the ever-honest Montgomery.

The servant looked from one to the other and then away, grimacing before he continued, "I understood, from what the marquess said, that the three of you hope to win brides of a certain nature."

"He means heiresses," said Max. "He means we are fortune hunters."

"I do not, Master Max," said Barton, puffing out his chest indignantly.

"Then what do you call it?" asked Montgomery quietly.

"First of all, each of you is a gentleman, a man of property, are you not?" When they had nodded, he said, "Then you are not fortune hunters. Marriages such as the ones you seek are made all the time, matching fortunes with estates, money with investments. It is nothing to be ashamed of."

"Good, then we need not spend any more of the marquess's money on clothes," said Montgomery.

"No, I mean, *yes*, sir, you must. It is important for each of you to appear in the best light, or your mission might fail."

"Rather like a military campaign," said Tristram. "You should relish that aspect of it, Maxwell. I mean, you are forever reading about battles and soldiers."

"Only because I cannot be one," he replied with a scowl.

"But you do see my point," said the manservant.

"Yes, yes. Very well, Barton, we will each order a few more coats and such," said Montgomery, his pride swallowed as he thought of Miss Landis. He would do whatever was necessary to win her hand.

There was a knock on the door and Barton answered it, accepting the note from the footman and returning to hand it to Montgomery.

"It is from the marquess," he said, scanning it and handing it to Maxwell. "An invitation to join him in his box at the theater tonight. How fortuitous."

"Are we going to the theater, then?" asked Tristram.

"Of course we are, which you would know if you came down out of the clouds and paid heed to the conversation around you," said Montgomery.

"Yes, Monty has been summoned by Miss Landis to visit her during the interval. She will be in Lord Benchley's box."

"Who the devil is Lord Benchley?" asked Tristram, taking the note from Max and scanning it briefly.

"Evidently, Lord Benchley is Monty's stiffest competition for Miss Landis's hand," said Max, winking at his little brother.

"That's enough of that, Maxwell," came the eldest's repressive response. Montgomery walked to the door of the tiny sitting room.

Tristram sat back in his seat and studied Montgomery a moment before commenting, "And here I thought you were a bit of a slow top, big brother. I had no idea you were such a quick study."

"Oh, bang up to the mark, he is," drawled Max.

Montgomery turned and smiled, picking up first one pillow from the settee and launching it at Tristram's head before ducking and sending the next one into his twin's face. Books, pillows, and even a muffin flew — anything at hand that could be used as a missile. Suddenly, there was a crash as one projectile hit the tray of glasses.

Barton hurried in, only to find his masters sitting quietly, each in his own chair. Strolling toward the tray, he looked from the shattered glass to each of his charges.

"I shall get a cloth," he said, his nose in the air.

When the door had closed behind him, Tristram and Maxwell fell into whoops, but Montgomery went to the tray and began picking up the broken pieces.

"Children," he muttered in a superior tone.

"At least we can hit our targets. It was you who threw that book."

"It was not," he declared, settling for a fierce glare at Max when Barton opened the door.

"Let me, sir. I have put away all your new things, gentlemen. I have also taken the liberty of laying out suitable ensembles for this evening's visit to the theater."

"Thank you, Barton. Sorry about this. It will not happen again."

The servant straightened and nodded regally, leaving the three men feeling very childish indeed.

Several hours later, they were picked up by the marquess's carriage for the short drive to Drury Lane. They were to meet the marquess at his box, and were surprised when he was not before them. They quickly forgot about the marquess, however, in their eagerness to study their surroundings and the other people.

It was only natural that three such handsome young men should draw attention, and they exchanged nods and little waves with the ladies in the boxes across the way. Max nodded to a group of loud young men who were seated in the pit of the theater. They waved back. Several even called a loud hello.

"Friends of yours, Max?"

"Acquaintances I met while out riding. A decent group of fellows. Up for a lark — anytime, anyplace."

Montgomery's smile broadened as Miss Landis entered the box directly opposite theirs, and he said, "One thing I've been wondering about. Why did Cravenwell suddenly decide to ask us to the theater — to share his box? I questioned Barton, and he said he didn't think the marquess had attended a performance in months."

"Who cares," said Max, leaning over the balcony.

"It has to be a coincidence, doesn't it?" said Tristram, who was busy drawing the theater.

"I suppose. I mean, it's not as if he could

have known about Miss Landis inviting us to visit her in Lord Benchley's box," said Montgomery, looking thoughtful. He focused on his lady love and forgot all else as the curtain rose.

He had only an hour to wait before he could join her.

"Excellent," said a rusty voice from the back of the box. With a shuffling of chairs, the marquess moved forward and sat down beside Montgomery. "Most satisfactory."

"Good evening, my lord," said the Darby brothers.

"Glad to see everyone is so interested in you," he replied. "That Landis chit — she'll be swimming in the money once her father snuffs it. He's young, of course, but time has a way of flying when you're busy living."

Montgomery's jaw tightened, but he held his tongue. So the marquess knew about his interest in Miss Landis. He cast back to that morning, when he had been telling Max about her. Barton had been in the room. He must be reporting to the marquess. Montgomery's eyes narrowed as he glanced sideways at the old man.

Cravenwell was a man of low morals, but he was cunning. He had to be — he was too wealthy and powerful. So why was the marquess taking such an interest in him and his brothers?

The marquess could not be described as a friend of his father's. He was more like a rival. His father was always trying to get the best of the wicked marquess, but he never did, of course. His father had yet to understand that the man who was desperate to win, rarely did. Instead, the winners were usually men who had no need of more fortune.

It made no sense. If his father had lost another large sum to the marquess, then why would the old curmudgeon be helping them? Yes, if all of them married well, they might be able to pay off some of their father's losses, but not a huge sum. Dowries were simply not that big — at least, not in his rather limited experience, thought Montgomery. Somehow, he doubted the elderly marquess was hoping to outlive Miss Landis's father. It was a mystery he wanted solved.

"It's time, Montgomery," said Max, nudging him in the ribs as the curtain fell.

"Oh, yes. If you will excuse us, my lord," he said.

"Happy to, Mr. Darby. You have business to transact," came the crude reply.

Montgomery would have spoken, but

Max dragged him out of the box and into the corridor. "No time for that. If we are to reach Benchley's box before it is overrun with her other admirers, we must hurry."

Montgomery and Max walked quickly to the other side of the theater, nodding to new acquaintances, but not stopping. Just before reaching their objective, they were waylaid by the talkative Lady Letitia. Smiling at Montgomery, she held out her hand. Before she could protest, Max took it and turned her, leading her a short distance away, introducing himself, and flattering her shamelessly. With his free hand, he waved Montgomery onward.

Taking a deep breath, Montgomery entered Lord Benchley's box. It was crowded. Beside Miss Landis was her cousin, Miss . . . oh, he could not remember her name. Clarissa Something. Next to her was the chaperone. And the man in the back would be Mr. Landis. That left two older, nondescript matrons. Looking at the hawkish profile of Lord Benchley, he guessed which one of the ladies was a relative of this gentleman. The other might be Miss Landis's mother. Since he could not throw people out of his way and get to Miss Landis's side, he might be wise to make the acquaintance of this lady.

Bowing low before the two matrons, Montgomery said, "Good evening, ladies. I believe we have not had the pleasure. I am Mr. Darby. Perhaps you are acquainted with my father, Viscount Tavistoke." Judging by the look the hawk-nosed woman gave him, she did know his father and was not impressed.

"How do you do?" said the other lady, extending her hand for him to bow over. When she smiled, he could see the resemblance with her daughter. "My daughter mentioned meeting you this morning. Oh, I mean, it was this morning that she mentioned meeting you last night," she added with a titter.

"Of course," he replied. "I am delighted to meet you, Mrs. Landis."

"And you. Oh, and this is Lady Hilda Vincent, Lord Benchley's sister."

"Delighted," he said, bowing again. Mrs. Landis was already turning to her husband and tugging on his sleeve.

"Mr. Landis, this is Mr. Darby, the young man Adele told me about this morning."

Mr. Landis looked Montgomery over from head to toe, then grunted something

99

and resumed staring across the theater.

His wife gave another titter of laughter and said, "Will you not be seated, sir? I understand you are just arrived in London, Mr. Darby."

Taking a seat, he said proudly, "Yes, I have an estate in Cornwall. Well, it is my father's, of course, but I take care of it." Let them know he was a man of property, at least.

"Humph," said Lady Hilda. "If the place is anything like that father of yours, it is run down and neglected."

"Now, Lady Hilda, I'm sure Mr. Darby is a very good steward of his inheritance."

"I try," said Montgomery, smiling at the woman he hoped would one day be his mother-in-law. He noted that Adele's father seemed to be paying attention, and he took this chance to paint himself in a good light. "I am terribly interested in the new science of agronomy. I am always reading about ways to improve the yield of my crops." Not that he could afford to implement them, he thought, but he wisely kept silent on that score.

"Fascinating, Mr. Darby. Isn't that fascinating, Mr. Landis," said his wife, beaming at each of them in turn.

"I don't hold with those new ideas," said

Lord Benchley, dragging his chair around and facing them. Holding out his hand, he added, "I'm Benchley. I believe we met briefly at Almack's last night."

"How do you do, my lord," said Montgomery, rising from his seat and sketching a bow.

The earl waved him back down and said, "What has worked for centuries is good enough for me."

"I agree with you to some extent," said Montgomery, warming to his topic. "I do not advocate throwing out all the old methods. That would be foolish. But have you read . . ."

Everyone else was forgotten as Adele touched his shoulder. "Mr. Darby, I did not realize you had called," she gushed before turning to her cousin. "Clarissa, only look. It is that charming Mr. Darby, come to visit us."

Clarissa obediently turned and smiled. "Good evening, Mr. Darby."

"Miss Landis, Miss Starnes." Whew, he had remembered in time. "You are both looking lovely this evening."

"You are too kind, Mr. Darby. Are you enjoying the play?" asked Miss Landis.

"Yes, it is very good," he replied, trying to remember the title of the deuced play.

He had been too preoccupied by Miss Landis's charms to take much notice of what was happening on stage.

"Mr. Kean's portrayal of Shylock is divine, do you not agree, Mr. Darby?" Clarissa Starnes looked at him pointedly, and he smiled at her, silently blessing her for the gentle reminder.

"Yes, I had heard of his excellent reputation in the role."

"I think his Richard the Third is even better," she said.

"Indeed, I hope to see that also while I am in London," said Montgomery, once again getting lost in Miss Landis's blue eyes.

"Will you be here for the entire Season, Mr. Darby?" asked this beauty.

"I certainly plan on it. I may miss my home, but I have discovered London has certain attractions of its own." Suddenly aware of his audience, Montgomery looked away, his gaze falling on Miss Starnes.

"Mr. Kean's performances, for one?" she said, pulling him out of the flames of clumsiness.

"To be sure. And then there is Almack's," he added, wishing he had visited some of the museums so he would not sound quite so shallow.

But once again, Miss Starnes came to his rescue. "So you enjoyed last night at Almack's, sir?"

"Yes, the scintillating conversation, the dancing."

"But did you not find the refreshments appalling?" asked Miss Landis, batting those wide blue eyes at him.

Montgomery's voice came out in a squeak, "Perhaps they are not the best in the world, Miss Landis."

"Nevertheless, you will attend Almack's again, will you not?" she asked, watching him intently.

"If you will be there," he said, his voice little more than a whisper — and a good thing, since it was lost in the sound of the curtain rising and a general scraping of chairs as everyone hurried to return to their seats.

"I should be going. Good evening, ladies and gentlemen," said Montgomery, rising and executing a creditable bow before hurrying back to his own box.

When he arrived, the marquess cackled, "Have you swept her off her feet yet?"

"I am certainly trying," murmured Montgomery. Looking around the box, he asked, "What has happened to my brothers?"

"That young one didn't come back so I sent the other one to find him. I don't mind telling you, I think he will be a sore disappointment to your old father."

"I take leave to tell you that you are wrong, my lord," said Montgomery, one brow rising skyward, a sure sign that he was angry. The marquess paid no heed.

"Time will tell. You, however, need to make a push if you're to win Miss Landis away from Benchley. He is stiff competition indeed."

"I think I am up to the challenge."

Squinting, the old man muttered something under his breath. Then he snapped his bony fingers and said, "I have it. You must give Miss Landis a present of such magnificence, she will not be able to ignore you."

"I can hardly do that, my lord. First of all, I don't have the funds. And secondly, she would not accept an expensive gift."

"You think not? In my experience, the ladies love little baubles, the more expensive, the better."

"Pardon me for speaking bluntly, sir, but I believe the females of your acquaintance could not strictly be termed ladies."

Expecting a set-down, Montgomery was surprised when the old man started cackling, each sequence followed by a wheezing sound as the old man caught his breath.

By the time he had finally recovered, Max and Tristram had rejoined them, and the marquess, beaming at the brothers, chortled, "Devil take me, I don't know when I've been more amused. Sponsoring the three of you is proving better than the play!"

Friday morning brought a bout of showers, but by afternoon, the skies were clearing, and everyone who was anyone headed for Rotten Row — to see and be seen.

Adele and Clarissa were no exception, though Clarissa's inclusion was not of her own choice. Her cousin had aspirations to create a stir by driving a high perch phaeton behind a pair of prime bits of blood. So far, she had had to settle for the more sensible curricle her father sometimes drove. Still, Clarissa had no confidence in her cousin's abilities, and she clung to the side with one hand while holding onto her bonnet with the other.

"I do wish you would calm down," snapped Adele when Clarissa gasped over another of her quick turns. "Have I ever turned us over?"

"No, but you have not done with trying," came Clarissa's dry comment. "And why must we bring poor Petey with us?"

"I don't mind," said a little voice behind them.

"Petey, are you all right?" demanded Clarissa.

"I'm fine, Miss Starnes," said the little boy. "I like dressing up in my finery an' riding on back here. Whoa! That was a big rock!" he exclaimed when the carriage jumped.

"Adele, you are putting that child's life in danger."

"Fiddlesticks! You love it, don't you, Petey?"

"Yes, miss!" called the child.

"There, you see? Oh, there is Mr. Darby," said Adele, slapping the ribbons against the horses' rumps, causing them to leap forward.

"Not so fast, Adele," said Clarissa.

"Do not . . . oh, only see what you have made me do!" declared Adele as the whip fell from her hand. She began sawing at the mouths of the horses, but to no avail.

The horses broke gait and began to gallop, their strides lengthening. Clarissa could not stop herself from letting out a shrill, "Help!"

Suddenly, a huge black charger appeared on one side of the team. Seconds later, another rider arrived on the other side. The Darby brothers gradually slowed their mounts, and Adele's wild-eyed team calmed down, slowing along with them. Max reached out and pulled on the ribbons until the team finally stopped.

Clarissa hopped out of the carriage, unassisted and fighting mad. "How dare you risk our lives like that, Adele? You pretend to be a whip, but you're nothing but a ham-fisted . . . Petey, are you all right?" The white-faced tiger nodded, and Clarissa continued, "Adele, I . . ."

"Miss Starnes, you are frightening the horses," said Max, grinning down at her even as he lectured her. She glared, first at him and then at his brother, Montgomery, who had dismounted.

"You must be exhausted after your ordeal, Miss Landis. Would you like me to drive you home?" asked Montgomery, standing beside the curricle and staring up at Adele like a paperskull.

Adele burst into noisy sobs — on cue, as always.

Stamping her foot, Clarissa turned on her heel and stalked away. How dare he? How dare he take Adele's side, when she was the reason the horses had run away with them in the first place?

Run away. No, it was more likely that Adele had allowed them to have their heads when she spied the Darby brothers. It would be just like her, thought Clarissa, grinding her teeth.

"Miss Starnes, how good to see you again," said the other dark-haired Darby brother, speaking to her from the back of his huge stallion.

She glanced up at him but said nothing, continuing on her way in an angry silence. Max Darby dismounted and caught up with her, walking by her side without speaking. By the time they had reached the entrance of the park, Clarissa's temper had cooled, and she stopped, looking up at him and grinning.

"You need not escort me home, Mr. Darby. It is not far, and I will be fine."

"I am certain you will be, Miss Starnes, but I would be failing in my gentlemanly duty if I left you here. Do you mind my walking with you?"

"Of course not. I appreciate it, especially since I know you prefer riding."

He glanced over his shoulder, smiling at Thunderlight and nodding. "Indeed I do." Recalling his role as gentleman, he added,

"However, I much prefer walking with a beautiful lady, of course."

"I shall not question your truthfulness, sir, and I apologize for being so rude. I was angry with Adele. I should not have taken it out on you or your brother."

"Quite understandable. I am surprised you agreed to ride with her. It seems rather foolish."

"I had no choice." At his appalled expression, she said, "No, it was not like that. It is simply that, if I tell Adele I am unable or unwilling, she forces Miss Anderson to accompany her. Miss Anderson is too mature for such high jinks."

"Then I commend you for your foolishness," said Max. "I have often noticed that people who have no business handling horses often choose the most high-spirited horses. You, for instance, I wager you could handle that team with one hand tied behind your back."

"You are too kind, but no, I could not. I can drive a single horse in the gig, but I have never attempted to drive a team."

"It would be my pleasure to teach you, Miss Starnes."

"A delightful scheme, to be sure, Mr. Darby, but when?"

"In the morning. I daresay one or two

lessons and you would have the hang of it. What do you say?"

"May I think about it?" she asked.

"Of course you may. I say, isn't this your uncle's house?"

"Yes. Thank you for escorting me home. You have saved me from total ruin. Walking through the park alone, especially at the fashionable time of day, is simply not done," she said.

"It was my pleasure, Miss Starnes," he said, sweeping an elegant bow.

As Clarissa started up the steps, Porter opened the door. Turning to wave at Max, she saw a footman from their neighbor's house come flying down the pavement, skidding to a halt in front of Mr. Darby. Clarissa watched as the footman reluctantly took charge of Thunderlight while Mr. Darby walked into the Marquess of Cravenwell's house.

"What are you doing with that one?" demanded the marquess, looking up from the papers strewn across his desk.

"I beg your pardon, sir?" said Max, his brow clearing when he noticed the study's windows overlooked the street.

"That one. She's the wrong one. She hasn't a feather to fly with," said the old man. Frowning, he picked up a pair of spectacles and put them on. "You're not even the right brother."

"I haven't a clue what you are talking about, my lord."

"No, you wouldn't. You are too busy riding that brute of a stallion of mine. Just see that you don't fall and break your neck. You are of no value to me dead."

"I shall do my best," came Max's dry retort.

"Good, now what about your brother? As I understood it last night, he was the one courting the girl next door, not the cousin, but the daughter."

"I believe that is correct, my lord, but I fail to see why it is any concern of yours."

"No concern of mine? Listen to me, my fine rascal, why do you think I'm footing the bill for your Season? For the money. And if you don't meet with success, who is going to suffer?"

"How could our finding brides possibly affect you?" said Max with a shudder of revulsion as the old man started to shake his bony finger at him.

"Not me, you fool. Your father. I'll have him thrown into debtor's prison if you three cannot pay me what he owes me, as well as the blunt I'm shelling out on the three of you. Just remember that when you start looking over this year's crop of girls. Now, let yourself out, and keep quiet about this. It's just between you and me, do you hear?"

Without another word, Max left the marquess and hurried outside, into the sunshine. Everything was suddenly crystal clear. They had wondered why the marquess was sponsoring them. Now he knew, and he was not supposed to tell the others.

That was fine by him. He didn't want to tell his brothers that their father had set them up, that their father had practically sold them into slavery.

No, he would not tell Tristram and Montgomery. He didn't even want to think about it himself!

Max took the reins from the footman and swung up on Thunderlight. Turning the horse, he rode through the streets until he realized he had left the city behind. Green meadows lay before him, and he put the big stallion through his paces.

With the wind whipping the long, black mane into his face, Max shouted, "Devil take me, Thunder!"

When he had brought the horse to a trot again, he patted his foaming neck and said, "With your help, old boy, I just might be able to solve all our problems — even my reprobate father's!"

Clarissa shooed the cat off her bed and sat down to remove her half-boots. Drawing back the coverlet, she fell face down on the feather mattress.

"Meow, prrrr," said the cat, hopping back on the bed.

Clarissa grabbed the old cat and hugged it fiercely. It rubbed its nose against her chin and purred louder still.

"Tell me, Humphries, why you men are so stupid. You can have a perfectly lovely person staring you right in the face and go all silly over the mere mention of some prettier but not-so-perfect female's name."

Sitting up, Clarissa crossed her legs and pulled the fat cat onto her lap. "Oh, I grant you, golden hair and china blue eyes are to be desired. And she has an excellent figure. But compared to plain old me, for sheer personality and amicability, Adele simply doesn't hold a candle to me."

"Meow," he replied, standing on tiptoe to rub her chin again.

"Precisely. At least you are aware of my many excellent attributes. Now, what shall I do to make certain the Honorable Montgomery Darby is aware of them? Montgomery. Such a mouthful. And there are too many Mr. Darbys to use that. I shall call him Monty. Yes, yes, only in private, just between you and me.

"Why shouldn't I have just as much of a chance with him as Adele? According to Porter, who had it from the footman, who had it from the upstairs chambermaid at the wicked marquess's house, Monty is quite flush in the pocket. He won't care that the only thing I bring to our marriage is my late mother's pearls and a good heart. Well, there is more, of course, but I am too much of a lady to enumerate those things, even to you, my dear fellow.

"So, I say, let the games begin. Besides, Adele won't want him anyway. She wants a title to go along with all those thousands Uncle Clarence is settling on her, not to mention the estates, and the . . ."

Clarissa pulled the covers up and lay back on the pillow with a sigh.

"I'm going to have my work cut out for me, Humphries. I simply must get my rest."

"Tristram, why don't we wait and go next week? It has been raining all day, and the grounds are bound to be muddy," said Montgomery. "Vauxhall will still be there next week."

"I don't want to wait. I put it off last week when you said I wasn't dressed properly. Well, now I am fine as fivepence, so I am going. If you and Max don't want to accompany me, I shall go alone. I am not a child, you know."

"Don't be a fool, brat. We are all children when it comes to knowing our way around London," said Maxwell. "Even if you manage to find your way there without being taken for a flat and robbed, you'll not have a good time all alone."

"And you'll never grow up if you listen to Barton all the time and only attend the entertainments he deems suitable. The walls are beginning to close in on me."

"Then why don't we go across the street to the coffeehouse. . . ."

"Not the coffeehouse! I have drawn every member of the landlord's family and most of the patrons. I must get out to see other sights — alone, if necessary."

"Very well, we will go together, but we are only going for the fireworks display and spectacle. Agreed?" said Montgomery. "At any rate, I believe one has to reserve a box in the Rotunda and order supper ahead of time."

"I don't care about all that. Thank you, Montgomery," said Tristram. "I will get my new sketchbook and pencil."

"And you, Max? Are you going to change?"

"Don't see why. We're not going for the supper or dancing. Might as well keep on my boots and riding gear. Besides, we're going by road, right? You know I get sick in boats."

"Very well. I'll send word to the stables. It will have to be a carriage, though. Tristram isn't likely to ride on horseback, especially at night."

"Deuced nuisance, this habit of his. Maybe we should make him ride. Maybe he could learn to like it."

"Not likely," said their younger brother, coming back in the room. "If I didn't like it in the country, what makes you think I'll like riding here where there are all manner of distractions to spook one's beast? No, thank you. If I can't walk there, it's the carriage for me."

Max put his arm around his brother's neck and wrestled him into submission, saying, "Just don't get sick in the thing, or you will be the one cleaning it up."

An hour later, the Darby brothers descended from the carriage and entered the pleasure gardens of Vauxhall. They followed the throng of people heading inside, unaware that they were going down the Grand Walk that led straight to the supper boxes and the Rotunda where a wooden floor had been built for dancing.

"Excuse me, sir, but which way is the waterfall?" asked Tristram of a large man dressed in a homespun suit.

"Just veer left at the end of the row, young gentleman," said the man, giving Tristram a big smile.

"Thank you. Max, I'm going to shake free of this crowd and see the waterfall."

"Go ahead. We'll catch you up there."

Montgomery and Maxwell paused at the edge of the Rotunda, gazing about them in awe at the structure and the people. On a platform on one end, a group of musicians were playing, and several people had taken to the dance floor.

"Looks like the right sort of place to be, when we have more acquaintances," said Max. "I think Barton is right about hiring a dancing master, Monty. I could use some more practice before asking a young lady."

"Did you not waltz at Almack's?"

"No, I was too afraid of disgracing myself. Perhaps we can get someone next week," said Max, who was usually overly confident. Poking his twin in the ribs, he said, "Only look, there is Miss Starnes. I wonder if her cousin is here."

"Yes, she is here, dancing with Benchley," said Montgomery, staring at the couple as they passed close by. "Isn't she the most beautiful girl you have ever seen?"

Max chuckled and agreed. "Undoubtedly, but we should move along. We're blocking the way."

"You go on. I am going to stay right here for a while," said Montgomery, leaning against a column. "I will meet you and Tristram in half an hour at the cascade."

Montgomery settled back, content to watch the dancers twirling around in each other's arms. He felt a fire in the pit of his stomach each time the beautiful Miss Landis passed by. She was so graceful, so perfect in every way.

His face grew flushed as he thought about his next opportunity to waltz with her. He would practice with the dancing master and dazzle her with his grace.

"Good evening, Mr. Darby," said a voice at his shoulder.

Looking down, he frowned, loath to leave his daydreams behind. Then he recognized Miss Landis's cousin and smiled. "Good evening, Miss Starnes."

Studying him as he watched her cousin's

progress around the dance floor, she said softly, "I saw you standing here and thought you might like to join our party."

His dark eyes gleamed with excitement, and he said fervently, "It would be an honor."

Offering her his arm, he led her in the direction she indicated. Montgomery was suddenly very relieved that he had decided to change out of his riding gear and into his evening clothes. With a bit of luck, he might even have a dance with Miss Landis.

Before they could even reach the boxes, his hopes were dashed. The music ended, and a bell rang. Everyone in the boxes began to rise, moving toward the exits.

"Oh dear, it is time for the spectacle. Might I trouble you to accompany me, Mr. Darby? We must hurry if we are to catch up with my aunt and uncle."

"Of course," he replied, walking slightly in front of her to clear a path.

"Do you see them?" he asked as the crowd began to look heavenward, and a shower of sparks lit the skies.

"There they are," said Miss Starnes, hurrying along the wide path. Suddenly, she stopped and turned, peering down one of the many darkened paths.

"What is that?" she said, taking a step or

two down the dark path.

"Miss Starnes, I don't think . . ."

"Oh no, look! That poor man!" she exclaimed, tearing herself away from Montgomery and rushing headlong down the path, all the while shrieking, "Stop that, you! Stop, I say!"

" 'Ere now, wot's we got 'ere, me lovely. Come t' save th' poor little bloke. Come to play with 'Enry, 'ave you?"

"Take your hands off me!" shouted Miss Starnes, beating the man's head and shoulders with her fan.

It was a losing battle, until suddenly, she felt gentle hands lift her away. Looking back at her attacker, she saw him fly through the air, landing with a loud "Omph!" He scrambled to his feet and fled with his companions.

"Miss Starnes, are you all right? Whatever possessed you to do such a foolish thing?" Montgomery demanded, frowning fiercely at her.

"I saw that poor boy there, and . . . oh, I . . . I . . ." Clarissa Starnes dissolved into tears, her slender shoulders shaking.

Flustered, Montgomery's mouth dropped open. Uncertain what to do, he patted her shoulder twice and said, "There, there." He was saved from further action when the figure on the ground moved and sat up, moaning as he rubbed his head.

Forgetting about Miss Starnes's hysteria, Montgomery shouted, "Tristram! Are you all right, boy?" Rushing to his brother's side, he began an examination of bruised arms and legs.

"I'm fine, just bruised," said Tristram, pushing away Montgomery's hands and then feeling around on the ground. "Damn their eyes! They've taken my sketchbook!"

"Is that all you care about?" said Montgomery, hauling his brother to his feet, completely ignoring Miss Starnes's sobs.

"Well, I had just finished half a dozen excellent drawings when they jumped me."

"What the devil were you doing out here in the dark?" demanded his brother.

"Well, I wasn't in the dark until they dragged me out here, now was I?" said Tristram. "Monty, who's that?"

"That? Oh, Miss Starnes, my manners! Allow me to present my other brother to you. This is Tristram, whom you saved but a few minutes ago."

"Saved?" said Tristram.

"Certainly, you lobcock. If she hadn't heard the ruckus, I daresay those ruffians would have done more harm than steal your sketches. And here she is, crying her eyes out, frightened half to death, and we're talking about sketches and such," said Montgomery, once again patting Miss Starnes's shoulder twice.

"I'm not, you know," she managed to say, lifting her face so that the moonlight showed the tears on her cheeks and the laughter in her eyes.

"I beg your pardon?" said Tristram politely.

She smiled. "I am not crying. I am laughing. It is quite easy to see that your brother is completely disconcerted by a woman's tears, and I was upset at first. Are you certain you are quite all right, Mr. Darby?"

"I'm fine, thank you. And thank you for saving me."

"What's going on here? You are missing everything!" exclaimed Max. "Oh, Miss Starnes. Good evening. Delighted to see you again."

"Good evening, Mr. Darby," she said, starting to giggle.

Montgomery grimaced at this and said, "Max, take Miss Starnes back to her aunt and uncle, won't you? I'm going to help Tristram find his hat, and we'll meet you back at the carriage. I think we have had enough excitement for one evening. Miss Starnes, if you will permit, I shall call on you in a day or two, to make certain you have come to no lasting harm."

"Please do, Mr. Darby. My cousin and I receive our guests at three o'clock most afternoons."

Brightening, Montgomery said softly, "Your cousin? Oh, yes, I had forgotten. Then we will certainly call. Good evening, Miss Starnes."

As Max led Miss Starnes away, Tristram asked, "Have you any idea how the mere mention of this cousin makes your face go all foolish?"

"And why not? She is the prettiest young lady in all of London," breathed Montgomery. "If you and Max would stick by my side when we go out, you would have met her already."

"Oh, I saw you with her at Almack's, remember?"

"Yes, but you must meet her. She is an angel."

"If you say so, Montgomery."

"And I do," he replied.

When they were back in their snug rooms, sipping a hot punch which Barton had whipped up, the three brothers discussed the growing stack of invitations. Barton had sorted through them, advising them on which ones they simply had to accept and which they could reject, if they were so inclined.

Max dozed on the sofa while Montgomery and Tristram slouched in overstuffed chairs, their long legs stretched out to the fire.

"Montgomery, are you certain you wish to offer for this Miss Landis?"

"As certain of anything I have ever done."

"I see. So your, uh, friendship with Mrs. Richland back home, that was all a hum?"

"We will continue to be friends," said Montgomery.

"You know, I was rather surprised when you agreed to Papa's scheme. I didn't think you would leave Darwood Hall, especially at planting time."

"It is because of Darwood Hall that I came along — that, and to keep you and Max out of trouble," he said, grinning at his youngest brother. "I thought that if I could find someone who might fit in at the Hall, I could justify marrying for money."

"And now?"

"Now, I would wed Miss Landis whether she were an heiress or not. I know I sound a right fool, and I have only known her a few days, but I cannot imagine my life without her."

Rising, Tristram touched his brother's shoulder, saying, "Then I wish you much success, Monty. Good night."

"Good night, Tris." Montgomery closed his eyes, savoring the image in his head of Miss Landis, smiling up at him, her blue eyes bright and shining.

No, he could not imagine going home without her.

Five

Clarissa stared out the window at the gray skies and stamped her foot. There would be no ride this morning. Turning back to her bed, she climbed in and pulled the covers up to her chin. She would just stay in bed all day.

Ten minutes later, she was up, dressing in a charming green morning gown with long, fitted sleeves that covered the bruises on her arms where the ruffian had grabbed her. Twisting her straight dark hair into a neat chignon at the nape of her neck, she put in several pins. She afforded her appearance a cursory glance in the glass before heading for the door.

Idleness had never been her besetting sin, and after spending the whole of Sunday resting in her room, she was determined to find something to do. From the kitchens, the odor of Cook's bread filled her nostrils. She entered, causing the pot boy and scullery maid to jump to their feet.

"Please, go on with your work," said Clarissa.

"Good morning, miss," said Cook, wiping her hands on her apron. "Would you like a bite o' bread with some sweet butter?"

"Why, yes, that would be wonderful, but I wondered if there was anything I could help you with this morning, Cook." She could see the pot boy and maid stare, their mouths dropping open in astonishment that someone would come looking for work.

"I am afraid not, miss. Th' bread is all baking, and I haven't started on the supper yet."

"Very well. I just thought I might be of use. Thank you," she added, accepting a large piece of warm bread that oozed with Cook's special sweet butter. Taking the treat with her, she made her way to the morning room where her uncle and aunt were breakfasting in silence. Not wishing to disturb them, she continued on, finding a quiet spot by the front window in the drawing room.

She sighed, wondering if he would call. He had said he would, and he probably would do so, since he had not had the opportunity to speak to Adele since Friday afternoon when their horses had run away with them.

Taking a bite, she dribbled butter down the front of her gown.

"Well, you've made a proper mess of yourself now, Miss Sobersides," she said to herself. "Oh, well. It is not as if anyone will see it."

Just then, she heard the front door open, and Porter said, "Certainly, gentlemen. If you will wait in here, I shall ascertain if the ladies are at home."

Jumping up, Clarissa looked for a place to hide. She was well and truly caught, she thought, glancing down at the greasy stain on her green gown and rubbing vigorously with her handkerchief, only spreading the drips to make an even larger spot.

"You should try hot water and a bit of soap," said the man watching her from the doorway.

"I would have if I had known company was going to arrive so very early," she said tartly.

"Good morning, Miss Starnes," said Tristram, walking past his brother and into the room, bowing before her.

Clarissa returned a quick curtsy and said to Montgomery, "I daresay Adele will not be up at this hour."

"We came by to see how you are, Miss Starnes, after your heroic efforts the other night," said Tristram, smiling down at her and causing her to blush at her rag manners.

"I beg your pardon, gentlemen. I am afraid I was discomfitted by your unexpected arrival and my untidy appearance."

"I don't see why you should beg our pardon," said the younger brother, covering for his older sibling, who was casting longing glances at the door. "We are the ones who are rag mannered. I told Montgomery that we were arriving too early, but he insisted that ten o'clock was an acceptable hour."

Clarissa chuckled. "For some people, it is quite acceptable. For my aunt, for instance," she added, gesturing toward the door where her aunt was entering the room.

Frances Landis's golden hair was changing to gray, but in the soft light of the drawing room, she could have passed for twenty. She gave each man a warm smile.

"Clarissa, you should not be in here alone with our guests."

"Porter did not realize I was in here," she said.

"Oh, and what is that on the bodice of your gown?"

"Cook's sweet butter, I'm afraid. Now

that you are here, I will go upstairs and change. If you will excuse me, gentlemen?"

"Will you not be seated, gentlemen?" said Mrs. Landis. "I have sent word to my daughter that you are here."

"That is very good of you. Allow me to present my younger brother, the Honorable Tristram Darby."

"How do you do, sir?"

"I am quite well, thank you. And I am delighted to meet you, madam. I must tell you, your niece is quite a hero."

"My niece?" asked Mrs. Landis. "I'm afraid I do not understand, Mr. Darby."

Montgomery tried to signal his guileless brother to be quiet in case Miss Starnes had not revealed her actions to her family, but it was too late. With a shrug, he rolled his eyes and listened.

"At Vauxhall last week. Montgomery was escorting her back to you when she happened to hear a commotion in the shrubbery."

"I was not even aware that my niece was in your company, Mr. Darby," said the matron.

"She saw me standing alone and was kind enough to invite me to join your party. However, as things turned out, I never managed to do so."

"Just so," said Tristram, the storyteller warming to his tale. "Miss Starnes, as I said, happened to hear a commotion and charged in, startling my attackers, because the noise she heard was me being robbed."

"Oh, how awful!" exclaimed Mrs. Landis, turning pale.

Montgomery looked around him for something to use as a fan. Not finding anything, he settled for patting her limp hand.

"Yes, it was awful, and I don't mind telling you, if it hadn't been for your niece's timely intervention, I might have snuffed it. But in she charges, without regard for her own safety, startling the ruffians."

"I was right there, ma'am," said Montgomery, taking out his handkerchief to wave it back and forth. "She was in no danger," he assured her.

"I don't know if I agree with that. I mean, the big one did grab her arms. . . ."

"Ohhhh," moaned Mrs. Landis.

"Enough, Tristram. Cannot you see that she is about to faint?"

"Oh, I am sorry," he said.

Just then, the door opened, and Clarissa stepped inside. In a glance, she took in her aunt's pale visage, guessed the reason, and noted that Montgomery Darby looked decidedly disappointed when he realized she was not her cousin.

"Clarissa!" Her aunt leapt to her feet and flew across the room, throwing her arms around her niece. "My dear child! Are you all right? What a frightful ordeal!"

"I am fine, Aunt," she said, putting a steadying arm around her aunt's narrow shoulders and leading her back to the sofa. "I really do not see why you had to upset my aunt with the details of our little adventure at Vauxhall," she said, frowning at Montgomery.

"And so I tried to tell Tris," he said indignantly. "But the boy was blind to my signals."

"I am not a boy," said Tristram, sitting back in a sulk.

"Tell me, my dear. Did the ruffian . . ."

"He grabbed my wrist and my arm, Aunt. That's all. A couple of bruises that will heal in no time."

"Isn't she a Trojan, Monty?" commented Tristram.

"Pluck to the backbone," he said, smiling at her over her aunt's head.

She beamed at him, and said softly, "I was only happy to be of help. Besides, it was you who sent them packing, Mr. Darby."

"That he did," said Tristram proudly.

"Are you feeling better, Mrs. Landis?"

Patting her hair, the matron straightened and gave them a weak smile. "Yes, thank you."

"Good. I would hate to think I caused you lasting distress."

"No, no, I am fine, dear boy."

Clarissa asked, "Did you ever find your sketches, Mr. Darby?"

"No, I'm afraid not."

"That is a shame. I was hoping they might have thrown them down."

"Evidently they did not, though what anyone else would want with them, I cannot imagine."

"So you are an artist, sir?" asked Aunt Frances.

"I enjoy capturing little glimpses of life as it happens around me," he said.

"And he is quite good at it," said Montgomery.

"Do you paint as well as sketch? I only ask because I have been wanting to have my portrait painted."

"My experience with oils is very limited, I'm afraid. I daresay I could not do your beauty justice, madam."

Montgomery shot his brother a look of astonishment which Clarissa intercepted. She grinned, and he chuckled, shaking his head at their shared amusement.

"My brother is too modest. His experience is limited, but his talent is enormous. Our mother passed away when he was born, but he painted three miniatures of her from the large portrait in the gallery. They are very lifelike — every bit as well done as the original."

"Why, thank you, Monty," responded his brother.

"You're welcome."

Clarissa said sensibly, "That being said, I'm afraid he would not have time during the Season. Nor would you have time to sit for your portrait, Aunt."

"That is true. I had not thought it out properly. But I shall remember, young man, and one of these days, I will send for you," she said, tapping his arm and smiling. With a quick frown, she said, "I cannot imagine what has happened to my daughter. I sent word . . . Ah, Porter, you have brought the tea tray. Wonderful. Clarissa, you will pour out while I go in search of Adele."

"Miss Landis sends her regrets, madam. She will not be coming down."

"And you mentioned our guests?"

"Indeed, yes, madam, but she was quite adamant."

Clarissa bit her lip to keep from laughing. Glancing up, she found Monty's gaze on her, his dark eyes twinkling. He might be in love with her cousin, but he was evidently not completely blind — not that he would hold her laziness against her. No, he would probably find it endearing. Men did not care for robust females, she thought glumly.

"I do apologize, gentlemen, but Adele is a delicate creature and needs her rest. I am certain you will understand."

"Of course, Mrs. Landis. Think nothing of it," said Montgomery, accepting the cup and saucer Clarissa offered.

They made polite conversation for the next ten minutes while their guests consumed their tea and small cakes. When they finished, they rose, bowing over the ladies' hands.

"Thank you for an enjoyable morning, ladies," said Montgomery, giving Clarissa's fingers a little squeeze.

When he straightened, he even winked at her, making her heart do a strange flip.

"You will call again, will you not?" asked Mrs. Landis.

"Thank you, madam. We would like that. Good day."

With that, the sparkle went out of the

room for Clarissa, and the day returned to its former rainy, dreary state.

"What charming gentlemen," said her aunt. "I can quite understand why Adele refused to give her consent to Lord Benchley after meeting Mr. Darby, Mr. Montgomery Darby. He is quite handsome and so gallant. His brother is quite entertaining, too, but he is much too young for Adele."

Clarissa shrank into her shell, nodding and murmuring when needed as her aunt continued to enumerate Monty's suitability for Adele.

"But here I am, rattling on when I have work to do," said the matron, rising and going to the door.

"Is there anything I can do to help you, Aunt?" asked the dutiful Clarissa.

"No, my dear. I must confer with Cook about the menus. Just relax and enjoy yourself. I daresay we shan't have any other callers on such a nasty day." Her aunt left the room.

"And I wish we had not had those two," she grumbled before stuffing a small cake into her mouth.

She washed it down with the tepid tea and sat back, leaning her head on the back of the sofa and staring at the ceiling. She jumped and sat up straight when Porter cleared his throat.

"Have you finished with the tray, miss?"

"Yes, thank you."

"Would you care for something else?"

"No, thank you, Porter."

He picked up the silver service and went out. Glancing down, Clarissa picked up a large square of linen from the floor. Her eyes widened at the initials, *M D*, embroidered on one corner. Smiling, she put it in her pocket and then opened a drawer in the table beside her, taking out a deck of playing cards. Pulling the small table in front of her closer, she laid out a game of patience and began to play.

"Excuse me, miss, but Mr. Darby has returned to retrieve his handkerchief."

"I am sorry to intrude, Miss Starnes," he said, looking down on her from his great height.

Clarissa groaned inwardly. How could she explain having pocketed his handkerchief?

"Are you certain you lost it here?"

"Yes, I pulled it out to fan your aunt, and now it is not in my pocket." He bent down to peer under the sofa and chair. Clarissa slipped the piece of linen out of her pocket and let it fall to the floor as she stood.

"I cannot imagine where it might be," she said, moving away from the sofa.

"There it is!" he said, picking it up and putting it in his pocket. "Odd. It was not there a minute ago." He straightened and smiled down at her.

"I . . . I am glad you found it. It must have gotten swept up in my skirts," she said.

"Yes, well, it's a good thing I returned," he said, glancing at the small table.

Her breath catching in her throat, Clarissa said airily, "Really?"

"Yes," he replied, bending over and placing a red queen on a black king. "You might have missed that move."

His grin was answered by a tight smile. "How kind," she said. Clarissa sat down on the sofa and resumed her game.

Montgomery looked bewildered and shook his head.

"Good day, Miss Starnes."

"Good day, Mr. Darby," she said, her head down as she concentrated on keeping her hands steady.

After a moment's hesitation, he left her in peace. Clarissa ignored the tears that began to fall on the cards, blurring the pictures until she could not distinguish one card from the other.

He had no idea the effect he had on her. He came into the drawing room, turned her world upside down — again — and had no earthly idea!

And why did he have this effect on her? she ruthlessly demanded of herself. She had had admirers, although they had made it plain a match was impossible since she had nothing to bring to a marriage.

The trouble was, this man didn't even admire her. Oh, they felt a certain closeness of spirit. His sense of humor was closely aligned with hers; that much was evident from the morning's conversation.

She could not explain it, but when he looked down that patrician nose of his and into her plain, hazel eyes, she felt a quickening, a feeling so deep, so intense, that it rocked her to the very core.

"So, two gentlemen callers in one morning," said Adele, trailing into the drawing room in her wrapper. Her mother, if she saw her, would be appalled.

"Yes, and you narrowly missed seeing one of them. Really, Adele, surely you know better than to come downstairs in a wrapper."

Adele stretched and looked down at herself with a shrug. "This wool wrapper is less revealing than most of the gowns we wear. Pray do not be so stuffy and move over."

Clarissa moved to one side of the sofa and collected her cards.

"You need not leave just because I have arrived, Rissa," said Adele, using her little girl voice and Clarissa's childhood nickname. "Tell me about Mr. Darby. Was he very disappointed that I did not come down?"

"He did not appear to be going into a decline."

"But he wouldn't, would he? Mr. Darby is a man of substance . . . not to mention fortune. How much did Penelope Pruitt say he was worth?"

"I cannot recall. A decent sum, I believe."

"My, but we are prickly this morning," drawled her cousin. "Why is that, I wonder? Could it be . . . no, do not tell me you have developed a *tendre* for the handsome Mr. Darby. Or perhaps it is for his strange little brother who jumps out from behind pillars and frightens young ladies."

"He most certainly does not. Tristram is an artist."

"Tristram, is it?"

"Mr. Tristram Darby. One cannot always be saying Mr. Darby. It would be too confusing," snapped Clarissa.

"So if I said my cousin had developed a *tendre* for Mr. Darby, you might agree, and I would still not know if it was for my Mr. Darby, or one of the other ones," said Adele, studying Clarissa as if she could divine the answer to the puzzle.

Clarissa looked her cousin in the eye and said calmly, "You might say it, but it would not be true. I do not have a *tendre* for either Mr. Darby, but I am tired of watching you toy with your suitors like a feline torturing a mouse. Mr. Darby — Mr. Montgomery Darby — seems to think very highly of you. He may even be in love with you, God help him."

"In love?" exclaimed Adele. "Hm, I wonder."

"You wonder what?"

"I wonder how in love with me he really is. After all, a man may say he is in love with you, but you never know for certain. I think I shall have to put Mr. Montgomery Darby's love to the test. If he is able to prove his love, then perhaps, I shall accept his suit."

"You are a cold, calculating . . ."

"Careful, Clarissa. Papa may keep you out of loyalty to your mother, his late sister, but there is no doubt, were it necessary to chose sides between us, whose side he would choose."

Clarissa stalked out of the living room and up the stairs, determined to remain in her bedchamber for the remainder of the day. Indeed, she wished she had never left it!

Both Sunday and Monday were rainy and dreary. Most of the *ton* remained indoors, out of the elements. By Tuesday morning, however, with the sun peeking out from behind fluffy clouds, the streets thronged with people.

The Darby brothers kept their appointment with Sharp and ordered more clothes. The poor tailor was in a tizzy, rushing here and there, hurrying to keep up with the avalanche of new customers who had discovered him since the Darby brothers had appeared in his creations. While he was busy with customers, his wife and two sons were busily sewing.

As he worked, he kept muttering, "It is those broad shoulders, you know. I knew all along that all I needed were these broad shoulders."

When they had finished there, Max sauntered off, saying something about seeing a horse, and Tristram said he needed to purchase more paper. Montgomery strolled toward the Landis house, whistling as he walked.

This time he would arrive at three o'clock, the time when Miss Starnes said the ladies would be *at home*. He had strained to catch a glimpse of Miss Landis at church services on Sunday, but evidently she had not attended. And Monday, his impatience had led him to call too early. It had taken all his patience to live through the long afternoon and night, waiting for the time when he might pay her a call.

He wore a bottle green coat and buff-colored pantaloons. His neck cloth was tied in the mathematical. He had surprised himself by discovering that he had a way with cravats. At home, he had kept it simple, but since arriving in London, he had learned to tie his cravat in several styles. Tristram, who was usually so creative, had given up tying them altogether and enlisted his or Barton's help to tie his cravats.

Montgomery paused on the doorstep, taking out his pocket watch and checking the time. Three o'clock on the dot. He lifted the knocker only to have it yanked out of his hand as the door opened.

"La, Lord Benchley, you are frightfully amusing. I . . . oh, Mr. Darby. How good of you to call. I am just going out."

"Afternoon, Darby. Good to see you again," said the earl. With a wave of his hand, his coach and driver swept down the street, stopping in front of the house. He offered his arm to Miss Landis and led her down to the pavement.

"Good afternoon, Mr. Darby. I hope you will call again sometime," said Miss Landis, throwing him a dazzling smile before allowing the earl to hand her up into the carriage.

"Good afternoon," Montgomery managed to say before the carriage sped away.

Turning away, his head hanging low, Montgomery's elbow was hooked and he was whirled around to find himself looking down at the pleasant face of Miss Starnes. Though she was the one who had detained him, she appeared a bit flustered, and he gave her an encouraging smile.

"I am glad you called, Mr. Darby, and I do hope you are not set on spending the afternoon inside," she said breathlessly, reaching up and straightening her bonnet that was askew.

"Now that you mention it, I must agree that it would be a waste of a dashed fine afternoon, Miss Starnes," he said, grinning at her. "Shall we go for a stroll?"

"That would be lovely," she replied. "Green Park is very close, you know."

"As a matter of fact, I do," he said, matching his long strides to her short ones. "I was hoping to speak to your cousin, but she was just going out with Lord Benchley."

"Yes, I know. One minute, they were sitting quietly, and the next, out they went. It quite took me by surprise."

"Then it was not planned before?"

"No, Adele had said nothing about going for a drive," she said, glancing up at him through long black lashes.

"Hm, that is interesting. Has she decided to accept Lord Benchley? I beg your pardon for asking such a personal question about your cousin, but you must know, Miss Starnes, that I have a particular interest in Miss Landis."

"I had guessed, Mr. Darby. And no, Adele has not yet accepted Lord Benchley."

"Then there is still hope," he said desolately.

"May I give you a bit of advice, Mr. Darby?"

"Please do."

"Very well. If you hope to win my cousin, you must sweep her off her feet.

Adele wants a bit of romance, a bit of the dramatics."

"Really? So you think I should do something outrageous?"

"Not too outrageous," she said with a charming, little chuckle. "I do not mean that you should kidnap her or anything of that sort."

"Good, because I am not the type of man to treat a lady in such an underhanded manner, especially the lady I love," he declared stoutly.

"I see," murmured Clarissa. "Well, you must think of something. Fill the house with flowers. Bribe the housemaid to leave a little *billet-doux* on her pillow every night."

"Miss Starnes! That is positively shocking. I would never stoop . . ."

"Then you will lose her to Lord Benchley, Mr. Darby," said Clarissa, giving him a look of sympathy.

"You know, Miss Starnes, I appreciate your trying to help me, but I must ask myself why you are helping me. You hardly know me. Or perhaps it is that you dislike Lord Benchley for some reason and hope to prevent him from wedding your cousin."

"Nothing of the sort," said the girl, lowering her gaze for a moment before lifting her chin to face him. "I do not dislike Lord Benchley, but I do like you, Mr. Darby, and I want to help."

They were almost at the entrance of the park when they heard, "Montgomery! Montgomery!" They turned as Tristram appeared, running toward them at full tilt.

"What the devil is the matter?" demanded Montgomery, grabbing his brother by the shoulders. "Has something happened to Papa?"

Tristram could only shake his head, his hands on his knees as he tried to catch his breath.

"It's not Max, is it? Has he done something foolish?"

Again that shake of the head.

"Then what the devil — oh, pardon my tongue, Miss Starnes — what is it, Tristram?"

Tristram thrust the crumpled paper he was clutching into Montgomery's hands.

Montgomery studied the sketch of a dandy, his shirt points so high, they were stabbing his chin while his breeches were plastered to him, leaving little to the imagination. Looking over Montgomery's arm, Clarissa giggled.

"It's one of your silly drawings, but I fail to see . . ."

"Look closely, Monty," said Tristram, finally capable of speech. "It's not a drawing, it's a print of one of my drawings with a caption I never wrote — 'More fashion than sense.' "

"Hah, good one, that. But I still do not understand."

"It's a broadside, don't you see? Whoever stole my sketchbook at Vauxhall must have sold the drawing to this . . . publishing company."

"You mean someone has been paid for one of your drawings, Mr. Tristram?" asked Clarissa. When he nodded, she took the broadside and studied it more closely. "It is no wonder. This is excellent," she said, handing it back to him.

"It may be excellent, but I was not paid for it. Some thief was, and that makes me furious. Not only that, but they have more of them! Remember the night at Vauxhall, when I was beaten and knocked senseless?"

"Then you must find out who published this and go to them and explain that your drawings were stolen," said Clarissa.

"Of course. Why did I not think of that?"

"Perhaps they will be able to retrieve your sketchbook if the thieves return to sell them more drawings, and then they will pay you for the drawings instead."

"There is only one problem with that, Miss Starnes. Look closely at the face of the man in this picture," said Montgomery.

After studying the drawing for a moment, Clarissa gasped. "Why, it's Lord Grant! I would know him anywhere."

"Exactly!" said Montgomery, feeling a glimmer of satisfaction that one of Adele's suitors had been made to look so foolish.

Tristram kicked the dirt with the toe of his boot, saying, "I never meant anyone else to see my drawings, you know. I'm afraid there are a number of them that would be better left unseen."

"Well, I am amazed, Tris," said Montgomery, rocking on his heels and smiling. "If anyone had told me your drawings would land us in the suds, I would have said they were lying. I always thought it would be Max, racing down New Bond Street, or some similar nonsense. Who would have guessed?"

"I am sorry, Montgomery. I did not mean this to happen."

"Of course not, but since it has, you must follow Miss Starnes's advice and seek out this publisher. Threaten him with some sort of legal action if he buys any more of your drawings from this blackguard. Then let him know that if he wants any more drawings, he will have to deal with you."

"Then you do not mind if I sell some of my drawings to this person?"

"Of course not. I hope you manage to earn a little pocket money. I am proud of your talent, but do make certain the faces are not recognizable."

"Thank you, Montgomery. And thank you, Miss Starnes, for pointing me in the right direction. I must seek out this publisher before more harm is done. Good afternoon."

Departing at a more decorous gait than he had arrived, Tristram retraced his steps, waving to them as he reached the corner and then disappeared from sight.

"You are full of excellent advice, Miss Starnes," said Montgomery, offering his arm again.

She opened her mouth, as if to speak, and then clamped her lips together, her expression inscrutable as she took his arm. Montgomery waited a moment before continuing their stroll.

The silence lengthened, becoming uncomfortable, and he cleared his throat.

"Have I offended you in some way, Miss Starnes?"

Heaving a sigh, she said, "Certainly not, Mr. Darby."

"Good," he replied, patting the little hand that lay on his arm. "I thought we were becoming friends, and I would miss both your excellent advice and your companionship."

She stopped and gazed up at him, studying his face a few seconds before her natural sunny expression reappeared.

"I would miss that, too," she said softly, looking away and continuing their walk.

"How long have you lived with your aunt and uncle? Are you just with them for the Season?" he asked.

"No, my parents were drowned when I was fourteen. My father had not thought to provide for me, so my mother's brother, Uncle Clarence, took me in. He and Aunt Frances treat me as their own daughter in every way. Well, except for the enormous dowry and vast inheritance Adele will receive."

He glanced sideways at her throaty chuckle, saying, "Do you resent that?"

"Certainly not. Uncle Clarence has promised to settle a small sum on me if I should wed. But Adele, of course, must come first. I really do not mind."

He led her to one of the benches that dotted the park and sat down by her side before commenting.

"Then no one has touched your heart, Miss Starnes?" he teased.

Her eyes flashed with amusement, and then the fire was gone as she continued to gaze into his eyes. Finally, she lowered her chin, and he wished he could lift it again, could try once more to read the silent message there.

"No," she said softly. "Adele must be settled before we can think about finding someone suitable for me."

"I think you are only repeating what has been said to you."

She looked up and smiled brightly, shaking her head. Montgomery felt that a door had been closed on him, and he had the urge to shake her, to restore . . . but what was he thinking? He had no right, no desire, to care whether Miss Starnes was sad or happy, content or filled with desolation.

"I am sorry about your parents," he said simply.

"Thank you. What of you, Mr. Darby? Tell me about your life in Cornwall."

"About Darwood Hall? It is a large

house, well worn and well loved, as far as I am concerned. The land is good and rich, not extensive, perhaps, but it is adequate to keep us all fed and clothed. I can think of nowhere else on earth I would rather be," said Montgomery.

"I understand. I was only a child, but I felt the same about the estate where I grew up. There is something about home, I suppose. It would not be the same now, of course."

"Who lives there now?"

"A distant cousin. I was fortunate my aunt and uncle wanted to take me in since he was young and did not wish to be saddled with a ward, but I hated leaving my home."

"Yes, home. Darwood Hall is home. I would do anything to keep it safe. Others may not see it, but it is priceless to me."

"You speak as if Darwood Hall had little value. Surely it is more valuable than that," she said. "Reports have it that you and your brothers are quite plump in the pocket."

"Do they indeed?" he murmured evasively. He had not counted on being asked to corroborate or deny the lies that the marquess had evidently spread about them.

"Oh, yes. But then I suppose you, like

other people who have money, never think about such things. That is the way of the world, in my experience."

"Yes, I suppose you are right," he said, feeling absolutely miserable. He had always prided himself on his strong sense of honesty. What the devil was he doing, pretending to be some great land owner?

"Are you all right, Mr. Darby?"

"What? Oh, yes, quite all right. Perhaps we should be going back. I do not want your aunt to worry about you," he said, rising and holding out his arm.

With a puzzled frown, she accepted his arm, and they returned to the house in silence. There, all was formal and proper, and Montgomery walked away feeling tired and depressed.

Six

"Where have you been?" demanded Adele when Clarissa walked through the hall on her way to the solitude of her room. "Porter said you went out walking with Mr. Darby, but that was ages ago."

Clarissa turned and nodded, her eyes glittering with anger. It was not the right time for Adele to pull caps with her. She had done nothing wrong. On the contrary. She had kept silent when she wanted to shout to that dear, dense man that she loved him, heart and soul. She had even advised him on how to win her selfish harridan of a cousin, and she had kept secret her opinions about everything that mattered to her in this life.

"Not now, Adele."

Her progress up the stairs was halted as Adele dashed forward and grabbed her arm, forcing her to turn around and look down on her.

"You did talk about me, didn't you?"

Clarissa glared.

"Good," said Adele, her eyes narrowing. "Oh, dear, I was right. You have developed a *tendre* for him. My, my, but this must be difficult for you."

Clarissa shook her arm free and continued upward to the first landing.

"Pray do not forget, Clarissa, that he is mine, if I want him. Either way, he is not for you."

"Miss Landis, I believe your mother is calling for you in the drawing room," said the butler.

"Oh, very well. What does she want now?" she grumbled, marching past the butler and entering the drawing room.

With a grateful smile for Porter, Clarissa headed for her room. After turning the key in the lock, she climbed into bed and pulled the pillow over her head.

The trouble was, everything her cousin had said was absolutely true. She did love him, and she was very much afraid that this Season would prove horribly difficult for her.

Thursday afternoon, as elegant as any town buck, Montgomery and his younger brother called for the carriage to make the journey to Richmond for an *al fresco* breakfast at Lord and Lady Forsyth's riverside estate. The weather had cooperated for this event with bright sunshine and warm temperatures.

After leaving Miss Starnes on Tuesday, Montgomery had been racking his brain for some outrageous deed that would so impress Miss Landis, that she would fall madly in love with him — or, at the very least, would choose him over Lord Benchley. He had come up with nothing to intrigue her, save trying to pretend an aloofness he did not feel. Knowing how strong his feelings were for the beauty, he doubted his ability to carry off this plan with any degree of success.

In the shadows of the carriage as they rode through the bright afternoon, Montgomery studied his younger brother, wondering if Tristram might help him hit upon some solution. He was quite creative about other things, why not about matters of the heart?

Clearing his throat, he said, "Tris, I was wondering if I might ask your opinion about something."

"Certainly, Montgomery," said his brother.

"Thank you. You are aware of my feelings for Miss Landis, are you not?" When Tristram had nodded, he continued. "Miss Starnes suggested . . ."

"Well, you can do no better than to

follow her advice. She is a great gun, isn't she?"

"Yes, but . . ."

"And really, she is quite a handsome little thing — not my type, perhaps, but quite attractive, don't you think?"

"Tristram, I did not wish to discuss Miss Starnes," said Montgomery, holding up his hand for silence when Tristram would have spoken again. "As admirable as she is, she is not the person I wanted to talk about."

"Oh, I beg your pardon. So what did you need my help with?"

"Miss Starnes let slip that Lord Benchley has already received permission from Mr. Landis to pay his addresses to Miss Landis."

"Bad luck, old fellow! Guess you'll just have to settle on someone else. What about Miss Starnes, for instance?"

His jaw clenching impatiently, Montgomery continued, "Not necessarily. Miss Landis has put him off, for the moment. Miss Starnes hinted that this might be because Miss Landis has feelings for me."

"Oh, I say." With a grimace, his brother added flatly, "Good show, Montgomery."

"Yes, but she also advised that I needed to come up with some plan to impress Miss Landis — something outrageous."

"There is always Gretna Green."

"No, I will not be party to an elopement, and you should not even be suggesting it."

"Very well, then what is your plan? You can count on me to help."

Montgomery heaved a sigh of frustration. "That is just the point, Tristram. I do not have a plan. I have yet to devise any plan, outrageous or not, that might impress Miss Landis with the depth of my feelings for her. I was hoping you might have an idea. Something creative and unique."

"I see. Well, let me think." Tristram bent his head, stroking his chin thoughtfully. With a dubious grimace, he offered, "I believe the ladies like flowers. You might send her several bouquets of flowers."

"I could, but Lord Benchley has the funds to match that action and more. No, I need something that is uncommon, something that comes from the heart, not the purse."

"Yes, yes," said Tristram. "What about doing like Sir Walter Raleigh and throwing your coat over the puddle?"

"Hardly sensible. What's more, I would be ruining a new coat, something I am loath to do."

"True. I say, Monty, are you certain you

really want to wed Miss Landis? I mean, she is very pretty, but I take leave to doubt her sincerity. She seems a bit cold to me."

"I will not hear a word against her, Tristram," came the steely reply. "If you do not wish to help, then I will think of something on my own."

"No, no. You know I would do anything to help you, Monty. Let me put my mind to it."

They fell into a thoughtful silence until Tristram snapped his fingers and said, "I have it! You must make her jealous."

"Jealous? That is hardly outrageous. Besides, I am not at all certain how to go about such a thing."

"First you must enlist the help of Miss Starnes. She will be willing to help, I am certain of it."

"Do you mean that I should court Miss Starnes to make her cousin jealous?" asked Montgomery.

"Of course. After all, she and Miss Landis are practically like siblings, and you know how much rivalry there used to be between us. Yes, Miss Starnes is the perfect choice to carry out our plan!"

"You may have something in that," said Montgomery, his frown clearing. "But I must be honest with Miss Starnes. I must warn her what I am doing."

"That is only fair. Then she will be able to help, too. You know, plant those little seeds of jealousy when you are not around. You should seek her out as soon as we arrive and put your plan into action immediately."

"Capital!" said Montgomery, relaxing against the soft squabs of the carriage. "I cannot wait to get started. Within the month, you should be wishing me happy."

Tristram glanced at his brother's smug expression and rolled his eyes. "I only hope I may," he said quietly.

The driver pulled to a halt, and they climbed down and were directed to the back of the massive house by footmen in powdered wigs and satin knee breeches. They greeted new acquaintances as they progressed toward a huge green and white striped tent.

"Good afternoon, gentlemen," said the Marquess of Cravenwell from a chair near the entrance. "I have been wondering when you would arrive, when my fun would begin."

A flicker of distaste passed over Montgomery's honest face and he asked, "Your fun, my lord?"

"Yes, my fun. What d'you think I come

to these boring affairs for if not to watch the three of you? And where is the other one? Maxwell?"

"Maxwell had a previous engagement, my lord," said Tristram when he noticed his brother's distraction.

Montgomery's eyes traveled swiftly over the crowd in search of his quarry — Miss Starnes. He had to speak to her and ask her permission to use her — misuse would be the better word, he thought — in order to win her cousin's hand.

Taking his cane and tapping Montgomery's arm, the marquess said, "Out chasing blue ruin and lightskirts, no doubt. Maxwell will never succeed in this venture. He is too much like that scapegrace of a father of yours."

Diverted by these accusations and insults, Montgomery raised one haughty, black brow and stared down at the shriveled man. Never mind that the marquess's opinions marched closely with his own, that Max had always been too ready to accept any dare that came his way. He could not allow any member of his family to suffer insult at the hands of this dissipated old man.

"I must insist that you withdraw that comment, my lord," he said. Tristram, standing behind Montgomery, watched this exchange with wide eyes.

"Or what?" demanded the marquess. Glaring up at Montgomery for several seconds, it was the elder man who capitulated, looking away first. With a snort of laughter, he said, "Very well, I apologize. After all, I have no desire to lose my entertainment for the Season."

Tristram expelled a sigh of relief, but Montgomery's aspect remained icy cold as he said, "If you will excuse us, my lord?"

"Of course," said the marquess with the wave of a gnarled hand. "Do go along and tend to your business."

Tristram dragged Montgomery away from the irritating old man as quickly as possible. "Come on, Monty. We have bigger fish to fry." When they were out of earshot, he said, "I do not understand why you allow that rum touch to affect you so. You are usually the cool-headed one."

"I cannot help it. The man is like a parasite that gets under a person's skin and sucks the life out of him."

Tristram chuckled and shook his head. "There are those who would say that is what we are doing, allowing him to foot the bill for our visit to town."

Montgomery had the grace to look uncomfortable at this, and he would have replied, but just then, he spied Miss Starnes on the other side of the wide expanse of green lawn.

"Excuse me, Tristram, but if I am going to put your plan into action, there is no time like the present."

"Of course. Run along."

Clarissa had watched him from the moment he had strolled around the house and under the huge tent. She had barely been able to discern his face when he was under the shadows of the tent, but she could easily identify that tall figure and those broad shoulders. Now, watching him approach her, his face bright and smiling, her breath caught in her throat. He was such a fine figure of a man.

Certain that he would be attending the breakfast, she had dressed with care in a new blue silk gown and had twisted her stubborn hair onto the top of her head, dotting it with tiny pearls. Around her neck, she wore her only piece of jewelry, her mother's pearl necklace.

Clarissa had steeled herself against this moment, even as she had spent extra care on her toilette. And she had warned herself that he would only have eyes for Adele, that he would not notice her at all. But here he was, striding across the green grass, heading straight for her, his dark eyes fixed on her alone. Her heart swelled with possibilities, and she smiled. Monty, her Monty.

"Good afternoon, Miss Starnes," he said, bowing over her hand before nodding to the young man and woman who were standing by her side, all but forgotten by her.

"Good afternoon, Mr. Darby. May I present Miss Violet Reed and her brother, Mr. Reed? This is Mr. Montgomery Darby."

"How do you do, sir?" they asked in unison before succumbing to a fit of the giggles. Clarissa gave them an indulgent smile.

Ignoring their amusement, the dutiful Monty said, "Delighted to make your acquaintance, Miss Reed, Mr. Reed. I wonder if you would be so good as to excuse us. Miss Starnes and I are planning a surprise for a mutual friend, you see, and I must confer with her in private."

"Certainly, Mr. Darby," said the young man. His sister just giggled up at Monty and allowed her brother to lead her away.

"You should not lie to children," said Clarissa, taking the arm he offered and allowing him to lead her away.

"They are not children, and I wanted to speak to you in private," he said gruffly.

Clarissa found herself being caught up by his urgency. "What has happened?"

"Nothing, and that is the problem," he added miserably, his manner changing like lightning from grumbler to forlorn little boy. "Since last we spoke, I have been considering all sorts of possibilities."

"Possibilities? About what?" she asked, the flutter of excitement in her breast being extinguished by the churning in her stomach.

"About what? How could you forget? You advised me to come up with some scheme — some outrageous scheme — to win Miss Landis's heart. I came up with nothing. I am wretchedly unimaginative, you know."

"No, I did not know." She placed her hand on his sleeve and gave it a little tug. "We should stroll along the riverbank or people will begin to wonder at our serious discussion."

"You are right, Miss Starnes," he said, looking down at her and smiling a pitiful little smile. "I hope you do not mind, but in the short time we have known each other, I have come to rely on your good sense, your friendship."

"I do not mind at all," she breathed.

"That is why I thought you might . . . . Actually, it was Tristram who had an idea about how I might win your cousin."

"Did he indeed?" she managed, wondering how someone whose heart had turned to ashes could still have the gift of speech.

"Yes, but I needed to inform you of it. I mean, it would not have been proper for me to simply begin courting you without your knowing why."

"And why are you going to be courting me?" she whispered.

"In order to make your cousin jealous. What do you think? Will it work?"

Clarissa wanted to tell him he was a fool if he thought such a hare-brained plan would succeed. She wanted to tell him she would have no part in it, that he would simply have to resign himself to a lifetime of heartache, knowing he had lost the one he loved. She wanted to, but she did not. It was only fair, was it not? Wasn't he consigning her to a lifetime of heartache?

Instead, she gazed into those dark, passionate eyes, the eyes that had the power of life and death over her heart, and she nodded.

"Yes, I will help, Monty . . . I beg your pardon," she exclaimed, covering her hysterical giggle with a cough and blushing a fiery red. That would give the gossiping tabbies something to talk about! "I don't know what came over me to address you in such a familiar fashion, Mr. Darby. It must have been the spirit of cooperation, but I assure you, it will not happen again."

"There, there, Miss Starnes. It is not a matter of such great magnitude. Besides, that is what my brothers sometimes call me. I see nothing wrong with it, when we are in private. I rather consider you like a sister, and hopefully, one day soon, we will really be related."

He beamed at her, and Clarissa felt her spirits plummet even farther into the bowels of the earth. How could any man be so dense and blind? Could he not see that she wanted to be anything but his sister? Could he not tell that she was head over heels in love with him?

No, of course he could not, and she was not about to tell him. He was too happy about the prospect of winning her cousin. And for her, she would go along with this mockery if it made his face light up with happiness.

"I think first, we should take out one of

the little boats and go for a sail," he said, eager to put Tristram's plan into action.

"I really don't want to, Monty. I'm afraid of water. I never did learn how to swim."

"Oh, of course. Your parents and all," he said, frowning slightly. "I promise you, Miss Starnes. You really don't need to know how. I am an excellent oarsman, I promise you."

He stepped into one of the boats. It rolled back and forth for a moment. She took the hand he extended to her and stepped inside, too. The boat rocked higher, and Clarissa threw her arms around his waist to keep from being pitched into the river. It was not deep at the shore's edge, but how humiliating to land in the dirty water.

"That's right," he whispered in her ear. "She's watching us already. Hah! This may work after all!"

Montgomery helped her sit down and then did the same. Facing her, he picked up two oars and pushed off from the bank. After a few strokes, he stopped, shaking his head.

"I do hope you won't mind, Miss Starnes, if I remove this coat. I am unaccustomed to such a fitted cut, and it is impossible to row this boat comfortably."

"Go right ahead. Do you need some

help?" she asked, intrigued as he began to shrug out of the tight-fitting garment. She leaned forward and helped him ease one arm out, then the other.

"Thank you," he said, picking up the oars again. Clarissa placed the coat across her lap and smoothed the soft fabric. A smile played on her lips as she watched him rowing, his muscles rippling beneath the fine cloth of his white shirt. He was still decent, of course, the most interesting part of his chest was completely covered by his cravat and snug waistcoat. Clarissa turned her face to the breeze to cool it.

When they were in the middle of the lazy river, Monty said, "We should be talking. Miss Landis is not going to believe that we care anything about each other if we sit here in silence."

Shaken out of her pleasant daydreams, Clarissa asked flatly, "What do you want to talk about?"

"I don't know. I hadn't any particular topic in mind."

"I see. Oh, I know. Did your brother Tristram ever find that publisher?"

"No, he did not. The man must have moved, and no one seems to know where he is."

"Not likely, since he would have to take

all his equipment with him. Perhaps Tristram should hire a Bow Street Runner."

"What, one of those people who go about catching criminals? But Tristram only wants to find the person who printed his drawing, preferably before he prints another one. Heaven only knows who may be the subject of the next one."

"That is why Bow Street could help. They often locate missing persons, and that is what this fellow is."

"True. Very well, I will tell him so."

"Good. Now that takes care of one brother. What about your other brother. Maxwell, isn't it?"

"Yes, Maxwell."

"I have not seen him since last week at the theater. Does he have some other interest that keeps him busy?"

Monty grimaced and shook his head, saying, "His interests are probably not suited to polite conversation, Miss Starnes. Except for horses. When I asked him if he was coming this afternoon, he said he had to see someone about a horse. Max is extraordinarily fond of horses."

"Oh, yes, he was most impressed by my little mare, I remember. Does he keep horses here in London?"

"No. That is, we have access to Lord Cravenwell's stables. We thought that was preferable to bringing our own mounts along."

"Oh, yes. It is such an expense. I am only glad Uncle Clarence likes keeping a full stable. Otherwise, I would have no opportunity to go out for a gallop on fine mornings."

"Hmm," he murmured, his longing gaze firmly fixed on her cousin who was sitting at a table with Lord Benchley and several other admirers.

Clarissa's temper was rarely allowed out of its box, but this was the outside of enough, she thought, glaring at Monty, who was looking more and more like a great, lovesick puppy. Dark brown eyes indeed!

She wanted nothing so much as to get away from him, but in the small confines of their little rowboat, it was impossible. Nevertheless, with an indignant swish of her skirts, she stood up to turn around and face away from him. The boat tilted, and she screamed.

"What the devil? Sit down!" barked Montgomery, grabbing her hand and yanking it.

"Leave me alone!" she exclaimed, ignoring the lurching of the boat and trying to regain her balance.

"Clarissa! Sit down!" he commanded.

She glared at him, but followed his order. With a haughty turn of her shoulder, she managed to convey her displeasure.

The danger of capsizing over, both of them noticed the onlookers lining the riverbank. Laughing and calling encouragement to Montgomery, they were highly amused. Among them, however, was one angry face.

"You know, Miss Starnes," said Montgomery. "You are probably the cleverest lady I have ever met!"

She turned to look at him, wondering what he was talking about now. Had she not put up with enough of his inanity for one afternoon? But he was smiling at her with such gratitude, she had to ask why.

"I was wondering how to attract your cousin's attention, and you hit upon it without any difficulty. I do wish, however, that you had warned me. We very nearly ended in the drink."

"So happy you approve," she said dryly.

"Oh, I do, my dear. I most certainly do. She appeared quite shocked by our lovers' quarrel."

"Our lovers' quarrel?"

"Yes, just like you planned. Good show," he said.

Clarissa thought that she could quite cheerfully take the oar out of his hand and send him over the side. Instead, she laughed, loudly and gaily. The people who had lost interest in their theatrics, turned around again. Montgomery grinned at her and winked.

"I think we should go back to the bank now," she said.

"Are you feeling seasick?" he asked anxiously.

"Yes, decidedly so," she murmured.

She watched as the strong, even strokes of the oars sent them skimming quickly across the water, bringing their little tête-à-tête to a close. When they reached the bank, the servants dragged the tip of the boat onto the ground. Clarissa stood cautiously and gasped when strong hands closed around her waist. He drew her against his chest and lifted her easily out of the boat before carrying her several paces to the green grass and setting her down.

"There you are, Miss Starnes. I will accompany you to the shade of the tent," he said.

"Clarissa, if you have finished making a spectacle of yourself, I want you to attend me," said her cousin Adele. Lifting her nose in the air, she turned on her heel and stalked away.

"I say, Miss Landis, that is no way to . . ." began Montgomery. Turning to Clarissa, he said, "She spoke to you as she would a servant."

With a shrug of her shoulders and an impudent grin, Clarissa followed Adele, happy in the thought that her cousin had finally shown her true colors to Monty — happy, too, that Monty had noticed.

She caught up with Adele as she marched past the tent and into the house where a suite of rooms on the ground floor had been set aside for the ladies during the breakfast. Continuing past several rooms, Adele entered the last room, sending the maid away before closing the door and turning the key in the lock.

"What do you think you are doing, Miss Hoyden?"

Clarissa smiled and cocked her head to one side, saying with maddening innocence, "I have no idea what you are referring to, Adele. I have done nothing you haven't done before. Or have you forgotten the time you made the very starchy Mr. Pitchly row you about the lake? I seem to recall you chose a very thin chemise and

175

white gown, so that when you fell in . . ."

"It is nothing like that! You are trying to steal my suitor, and I simply will not have it! Do you hear?" screeched Adele and punctuated her words with a stamp of her slippered foot.

"I imagine most of the ladies in the surrounding rooms can hear," said Clarissa. "Now, do please open that door and let us return to the breakfast."

Adele's eyes narrowed, and she rushed to the door, throwing it open and closing it behind her. Clarissa heard the key turn in the lock before she could reach it.

"Adele, do not be so stupid."

"You can just cool your heels in there for a while. Do not worry. I will let you out before the dancing starts."

Clarissa waited a few minutes to make certain her cousin had left. Then she began knocking loudly. The maid appeared almost instantly.

"What is wrong, miss? If you will open the door . . ."

"I would love to, but I seem to have misplaced the key," said Clarissa. "Do go and fetch the housekeeper. She is bound to have another key."

"Very good, miss."

Clarissa sat down on the chair in front of

a large gilt-framed mirror. She picked up one of the delicate bottles and sniffed the contents before applying a few drops of the liquid to her wrists. She smoothed her hair and then smiled at her image. One thing was for certain. This was turning into an exciting Season.

There was a knock on the door, and a matronly voice intoned, "Are you in there, miss?"

"Yes, I am here. I feel so silly to have lost the key," she lied.

"There, there, I will have you out in a trice," said the housekeeper.

Clarissa waited while first one and then another key was tried in the lock.

"Is there a problem?"

"I cannot seem to find the correct key, miss. I'm afraid I will have to have someone come and take the door off. It will take a little while. Will you be all right?"

"Certainly. I am fine. I shall simply have a little lie down while I am waiting." Clarissa walked over to a delicate satin chaise-longue and sat down, ready to put up her feet and wait. Looking around for something to read, she spied the tall windows that started almost from the floor. Rising again, she hurried across the room and smiled.

The window was one that opened, and it was only four feet off the ground. She had to struggle with it a moment, but finally, it was open wide enough to allow her to exit. Clarissa frowned at the sill. Suddenly, it appeared much higher off the ground than she had originally thought.

Leaning down, she peered outside, making certain no one was watching her progress. The window was on the side of the house, however, and tall shrubbery hid her from the other guests' view. Luck was with her, she thought, sitting down on the sill and swinging her legs outside. She would simply have to jump.

"Here, Miss Starnes. You are going to hurt yourself," said Tristram Darby, appearing from nowhere and reaching up to place his hands at her waist, swinging her down with ease.

"There you are," he said, smiling down at her.

"Thank you, Mr. Darby. That is twice today that I have been rescued by one of the handsome Darby brothers."

"Ha, ha. Now all you lack is Maxwell," he said, offering her his arm. "Wasn't it lucky I happened along? By the way, what were you doing just now, climbing out of the window?"

"I would rather not say, if you don't mind. The tale puts someone in a rather unpleasant light, and it would be unkind of me to tell it."

"Miss Landis, you mean," he said.

Clarissa could not help but smile and nod. "You will not tell anyone, will you?"

"Certainly not. I take it she was jealous of you and my brother taking a little sail?"

"Yes, I am afraid so. Your plan seems to be working only too well."

"Humph, I was afraid of that," he muttered.

Clarissa stopped and turned to face him. "What do you mean by that?"

The young man blushed and stammered, "I do not mean any disrespect to you, Miss Starnes, but I must confess I cannot like the idea of my brother ending up with your cousin. She is . . . oh, not evil, but definitely not worthy of my brother. There, I have offended you and shocked you, too, by my plain speaking." She bowed her head, and Tristram fished his handkerchief out of his pocket, handing it to her.

Clarissa shook her head and lifted her face. She was laughing so hard, no sound was coming out. Darby's look of alarm was quickly replaced by amusement as he joined her.

When Clarissa had control of her voice once again, she said, "You must not think too harshly of her, Mr. Darby. She is not so bad. Most of the time, she is very kind."

He raised a doubtful brow, saying, "If you insist, I shall not quibble with you. Still, she is not the sort of wife I would like my brother to choose. You do not know Montgomery the way I do. He is always polite, always reasonable. And compassionate? When the barn cat had kittens at Christmas, and one of them seemed to be stillborn, Monty took it inside by the fire, massaging its little chest until it started to breathe. Because the kitten was so tiny and weak, he had all of the kittens and the mother moved inside, too. That is the sort of man my brother is. Is it any wonder I would prefer him to have a wife worthy of him? Someone more like . . . you, for instance."

Clarissa shook her head and backed away.

"No, no, I do not necessarily mean you, Miss Starnes. After all, if he were going to fancy himself in love with you, I think it would already have happened. Now, of course, he cannot see anyone except for your cousin."

"Yes, I know. Only think of it this way,

Mr. Darby. Perhaps being wed to your brother, my cousin will become worthy of him." Even as she spoke the words, every fiber of her being was denying it vehemently.

"Perhaps," he said as they continued toward the back of the house and the other guests. At the corner, he said, "Here we are, Miss Starnes, and your secret is safe with me."

"I was just wondering, Mr. Darby, what you were doing, lurking in the shrubbery outside the ladies' withdrawing rooms."

He turned pink and took a step back. "I promise you, I had no idea that is what those rooms were being used for, Miss Starnes. You must believe me!"

"Calm down," she said, her eyes twinkling. "I was only teasing. But what were you doing?"

"I . . . I was trying to capture the scene, the entire scene, from a different perspective," he explained. "Here, look." He pulled his small notebook out of his pocket and showed her several drawings, each from the perspective of the side of the house.

"And these are from the other side. You see? I was trying to draw everything, and I could not get it right while I was standing in the middle of the scene."

"You really are very talented," she said, taking the notebook and flipping through the pages. She chuckled as she saw one of Mr. Pitchly, his nose in the air. Her smile softened as she came across one of her and Monty in the small boat.

She bowed her head, unable to speak. Tristram took the notebook and carefully tore out the sketch, handing it to her.

"You might like to have this," he said, "to remember the day."

"Yes, thank you," she said. "Wait, what is that one?"

"That? Oh, it's nothing, nothing at all. Just a mistake."

"Let me see it," she said sharply. The hand covering the next sketch fell, and she found herself staring into Adele's cold eyes. Sucking in air, she expelled it in a whoosh. Glancing up at Tristram, she said, "May I have that one, too?"

"You are not going to show it to her, are you?"

"Oh, no. I would never do that."

Reluctantly, he tore out this drawing too. Withholding it from her, he said again, "You promise you will not show it to her, or to Monty, either."

"I make you my solemn promise," said

Clarissa, accepting the paper and carefully rolling it up so that it fit into her reticule. "Thank you, Mr. Tristram. I will enjoy looking upon both of your drawings from time to time."

She took his arm and led him back to the party.

Seven

Clarissa found the remainder of the afternoon and evening delightful. The musicians moved inside at dusk, and the dancing began in earnest. She danced as often as she wished, and even persuaded young Tristram to waltz with her. After this, she led him to Miss Reed. This kind young lady was in the center of a group of young people embarking on their first Season, too, and she knew Tristram would feel quite at home.

Monty, she noticed, had learned that, if one did not wish to become the target of gossip, one danced with numerous partners. In between, he could watch Adele surreptitiously, but he allowed himself only one dance with her cousin.

It was after eleven o'clock when she happened upon him at the buffet tables. "I am feeling decidedly neglected, sir," she said loudly enough for others to hear. Then she whispered, for his ears alone, "Have you already given up on your plan to make Adele jealous?"

"No, but I did not want to make things too uncomfortable for you, so perhaps we should forget the idea. I felt quite badly after the way she spoke to you this afternoon, I . . ."

"Oh, pish-tush," she said with more force than necessary. Dropping her voice again, she said, "I am not worried about that, and I am happy to help."

"Are you sure?" he asked.

"Positive. Look, there she is." She picked up a grape and said, "Open your mouth."

"What?"

"Just do as I say." He opened his mouth, and she stood on tiptoe, leaning against his broad chest as she fed him the grape. "There you are, good knight," she said, causing heads to turn. With a simper, she led him to a secluded table.

Seated with her back to the other guests, Clarissa could gaze at Monty to her heart's content. He, after all, was ignoring her while he stared at her cousin, his expression full of misery. Clarissa twisted in her chair and spied Adele, who was laughing at something Lord Benchley had whispered in her ear. Monty groaned. After several minutes of neglect, Clarissa decided to take matters into her own hands.

"Laugh," she commanded.

"I do not feel like laughing," he said.

"I do not care what you feel like. If you

are going to use me to make Adele jealous, then you are going to do it up right."

"Oh, so that's your game," said the marquess, leaning heavily on his cane while a servant followed after him, carrying his plate. "You would do well to remember to keep your voice lower, miss. I am not the only person around here with excellent hearing."

"Thank you for the advice, my lord. I shall keep that in mind," said Clarissa.

"You are welcome." He waited while the servant dragged a chair up to their table.

"Our plan would work better, my lord, if Miss Starnes and I were alone," said Montgomery, glaring at the marquess.

"Undoubtedly, but I have to sit someplace. I fail to see why you dislike me so, my boy. Perhaps it is because I am too honest for you."

Clarissa's brow puckered as she watched the tense interchange between the two men. She knew the reputation of the marquess was black, but Monty's cold reception of his father's friend puzzled her. Tristram had painted his elder brother as a saint, but she had difficulty tallying this with his current behavior.

The marquess ignored them while he set about devouring the first layer of his plate.

Delicate pastries were shoveled in along with roasted duck, brussels sprouts, and poached pears.

After a few moments, he waved his fork at her and said, "It all goes in the same place anyway."

"I beg your pardon, my lord?"

"I know what you were thinking, you saucebox. You were watching me and wondering why I was eating the way I was. You, on the other hand, eat only one thing at a time. No sense in that, I say."

"Are you insulting the way Miss Starnes eats?" asked Monty.

"No more than she," replied the old man.

Clarissa placed a restraining hand on Monty's sleeve and gave an imperceptible shake of her head.

Again waving the fork at her, the marquess turned to Monty and said, "I don't see why you want th' other one. This one's just as pretty and a deal more sensible."

"Really, my lord, I cannot tolerate such discourtesy to Miss Starnes," said Montgomery.

"Ah, I see. Sorry, miss. Guess you don't have the funds the other one has. Too bad. You would suit admirably in every other way, though you've a deal more sense than this young jackanapes."

"That is quite enough," announced Montgomery, jumping to his feet. "The musicians are beginning to play again, Miss Starnes. Would you do me the honor of this dance?"

Clarissa favored the marquess with an audacious grin before replying, "I would enjoy it prodigiously, Mr. Darby."

With a wink, Cravenwell cackled, "Yes, time to get back to work, Miss Starnes. I will be along soon to see how the play turns out."

Monty took her arm and led her back to the ballroom. The musicians were playing a waltz, and she put her hand on his shoulder while he placed one hand at her waist. The dance floor was not full since most of the guests were still eating supper, and they set off, not worrying about running into any of the other couples.

"Monty," she whispered, keeping her eyes on his cravat. "The marquess's comments about you and me suiting except for my lack of funds . . . Are you, perhaps, not as wealthy as everyone thinks?"

"I was unaware that everyone thought I was wealthy," he replied tightly.

"Well, someone, perhaps it was the marquess, though I cannot understand why, but someone has spread the story that you and your brothers are more than comfortably plump in the pocket."

"I promise you that neither I nor my brothers are responsible for such . . . lies."

"Ohh," she said, lowering her head. "Then it is true."

"I will understand if you want me to take you back to your chaperone."

Clarissa's head jerked up. "No, certainly not." They waltzed in silence for several minutes before she ventured, "Hold me closer, Monty. Adele has just entered the room."

"I cannot do that, Miss Starnes. I will not endanger the reputation you have worked so hard to maintain, all for the sake of tricking your cousin."

Clarissa grinned up at him. She could have taken his dear face in her hands and kissed him at that very moment, in front of everyone, but she did not. Instead, she pulled him closer.

"There, that is better. Not so close as to ruin me, but close enough that it will be remarked."

"Miss Starnes . . ."

"Monty, I think it would be quite effective if you were to occasionally forget yourself and call me Clarissa, even where others might overhear."

"I could not. As I told you . . ."

"Yes, yes, but I think my reputation can withstand a bit of spicing up. Perhaps that is the real reason I am still unwed. Perhaps I have been too proper," she said outrageously.

"You are teasing me," he said.

"Yes, I am teasing, Monty. But it feels good to do so. Now, let us do a dizzying twirl so that I can squeal just as we pass Adele."

"You are incorrigible, Miss . . . Clarissa," he said, smiling down on her and tightening his hold even more as they twisted and swirled, dipping with the rhythm of the music, until their steps brought them closer to Adele, who was watching their progress, Lord Benchley at her side.

"Oh, Mr. Darby!" Clarissa breathed, delving deep inside and discovering the soul of an actress. "You waltz divinely!"

"As do you, Clarissa," he exclaimed, his dark eyes twinkling as he gazed into hers.

Clarissa thought she could die happy at that very moment.

The music eventually ended, and so did her dream. Monty left her with Miss Anderson. She was asked to dance the quadrille next by young Mr. Reed. The brilliance of the evening dimmed as she watched her Monty hurry to Adele's side, winning the privilege of dancing with her in the next square of couples. He winked at Clarissa when they passed, and she forced a smile, despite the fact that her heart was breaking.

The next two hours were a blur of partners. She could not remember with whom she had danced, nor did she care — anything to keep her busy so that she did not fall apart and disgrace herself. She would not give Adele the satisfaction.

At one o'clock, they were herded outside again for a magnificent fireworks display. Though it was early May, the night was chilly, giving the gentlemen an opportunity to place warming arms around the ladies' shoulders. Clarissa pulled her shawl more closely around her and started back into the house.

"Are you not going to watch?" asked the marquess. He had stationed himself just inside the door, seated on a small bench, still high enough to see over the people on the lower terrace.

"Of course," she said. "I simply wished to stay warm."

"Then come and sit with me," he said, moving to one side of the small bench.

"Very well, I believe I shall. I would like to speak to you anyway."

He held up his knobby hand and shook his head. "I said too much earlier. I am sworn to secrecy, and I should not have spoken."

"I would not ask you to break your oath, my lord, but I think I have a right to know one or two things."

"Such as?"

"Just how wealthy is Mr. Darby?"

"Why does it matter to you? Will you tell that cousin of yours to scare her off?"

Clarissa shook her head, and the old man smiled. "What would you do, if he were to ask for you? Would you wed a penniless man?"

"No," she whispered.

He gave that awful cackling laugh that made other guests look around at them, at her.

"Yes, you would. Well, more fool you, Miss Starnes. And Montgomery Darby, too. He's half in love with you already, but he is too blinded by your cousin's golden beauty. Just as well. He would never wed you, miss. He has reason enough to wed a fortune, even if the idea is distasteful to him. He would do anything to keep that precious estate of his in order. Hah!

Darwood Hall! A collection of rotting timbers and cracked windows."

"That is why he wants to wed my cousin?"

"That's it. I could have taken the place, you see, as winnings in a game of hazard. But I don't want the place. I have enough estates. I only wanted the money."

Just then, the silence of the night was broken by a loud pop and a shower of bright sparks lit the night sky.

The gasp of admiration covered Clarissa's distressed cry, "Monty lost his estate to you in a game of dice?"

"Not that young cawker. His father's the gambler in the family. If your Mr. Darby doesn't wed money, I'll have his father thrown in debtor's prison. What do you think of that?"

"I think you are despicable!" she exclaimed, leaping to her feet and hurrying outside to join the other sane people.

"Look, there's a boat in the river," shouted someone.

"It's a private barge," said someone else.

"Wonder who it can be?" asked one of the ladies.

"They say the Prince Regent likes to . . . no, couldn't be him," said the man with a wicked guffaw as the deck was lit by another round of fireworks.

Everyone on the terrace stared at the deck of the strange boat, which had torches on the rails. They could make out figures lounging on chairs, but nothing else. Another burst of fire and sparks lit the sky, but the noise of the gunpowder was overtaken by the collective gasp of the assembled guests.

"Oh, my, that woman is . . ." began a feminine voice.

Her sentence was finished by a robust, "Naked as a newborn babe!"

"A better figure than a babe," said another masculine voice.

Boom! Another shower of light, and the people on board could be seen clearly again. Scantily clad females squealed as their companions dumped them onto the deck unceremoniously.

"It's gone down in the hold!" they heard someone on board shout.

"Jump!" yelled some of the other passengers.

On board, women were screaming, standing at the rail, men were running to and fro, and the amazed guests were finally roused to action. Monty was one of the first to reach the riverbank, grabbing the closest rowboat and shoving off.

Tristram was next, but his brother waved him back.

"Have the servants bring blankets!" he yelled.

"I'm coming, too! Max is out there!"

"No, you're not," roared Monty, putting his back into his rowing and shooting across the water. "One of us should be here to greet him when he lands!"

Tristram shouted to the servants to fetch blankets and to start building up the fires in the house. This done, he turned to watch, fear in his eyes as he looked for his brothers in the chaos.

Clarissa ran to the edge of the water, her gaze following Monty's every move as he reached the barge. She could see the flames inside the barge as they perforated the hull, growing stronger with each passing minute. The people on board began to jump into the river.

Clarissa clasped her hands when Monty's little boat tipped on end as he hauled one of the barge passengers aboard. It dipped again as he pulled another one on board. Two more figures, huddled together, and he turned the overloaded rowboat toward the bank. She gasped when the boat was upended as someone else tried to climb in.

"Leave him," she whispered, even as Monty grasped the unfortunate fellow and pulled him halfway into the boat before picking up the oars again.

Then she was running to meet him, to help him with his cargo of soggy humanity. Without a word, Clarissa wrapped her shawl around the half-naked body of one of the females. Tristram helped each passenger out of the rowboat before shoving it back into the water.

Clarissa gasped and protested. "No, Monty."

"There are more people out there, and one of them is Max," he replied grimly. "I will be fine," he added, giving her a little wink before gripping the oars and sending the little boat across the river again.

"See that everybody wraps up in one of these," commanded Tristram, pushing a stack of scratchy blankets into her arms. Clarissa set about ministering to the needs of the survivors.

"Here, wrap up in . . . Max! Oh, thank God you are all right!" said Clarissa. "Tristram, it's Max!"

"Thank God!" shouted Tristram, continuing with his work.

"Here. Wrap up in this, Max," she said, putting a blanket around his shoulders.

He gave her a disarming grin, so like his twin's that it made her smile, and then shook off the blanket.

Handing it back to her, he said, "Not yet. I still have work to do."

Maxwell set about counting heads, making certain all his friends, and even their friends, were accounted for. He was waiting when his brother returned again with the last two survivors.

Half an hour later, the burned out hull of the barge rested on the muddy bottom of the Thames, while its crew and passengers clustered around the huge fireplace in the great hall of Lord and Lady Forsyth's grand mansion.

"Miss Clarissa, let's go home," said Miss Anderson wearily.

Clarissa gazed with longing at the far corner of the room where Monty was talking quietly with his two brothers. She would have given a great deal to be a part of that warm circle. With a sigh, she nodded and followed Miss Anderson and Adele to the front door.

"Clarissa, wait."

She turned to find Monty looking down at her, his face smudged with smoke, but as handsome as ever.

"You forgot this. Your maid might be

able to do something with it," said Monty, handing her her ruined shawl.

Adele grabbed the garment and tossed it away. "You are not bringing that home in my carriage after that . . . that female wore it."

Monty bowed over Clarissa's hand and over Miss Anderson's. Looking down his nose at Adele, he ignored her hand and turned to pick up the shawl.

"I will have this cleaned if at all possible, Miss Starnes. Otherwise, I will replace it. Thank you for your assistance this evening. And you, too, Miss Anderson. Good evening, ladies."

He turned and walked away. Clarissa's breast swelled with pride. Every inch the gentleman, she had never loved him more.

"Of all the insolent nobodies," snapped Adele, shoving Clarissa ahead of her as they left the house.

Clarissa awoke early the next afternoon, sore and stiff after the exertions of the previous evening. She had never been involved in such an exciting, terrifying event. The heroics of Monty and the others who had rowed out to help had thrilled her in a way she had never felt before — and she hoped never to feel again.

She lay back on the pillow and smiled, her thoughts on Monty and those rippling muscles. Best of all was the admiring manner in which he had looked at her — her, not Adele. Perhaps there was reason to hope after all.

Suddenly, Clarissa recalled her disturbing conversation with the Marquess of Cravenwell. If what he had said was true, Monty could not afford to switch his interest from Adele to her. But surely the marquess was exaggerating. How could the old man know so much about the Darby brothers' inheritance anyway? Cravenwell never left London.

Still, Clarissa knew she needed to find out for herself what Monty's financial situation was. Tristram! She would probe him and find out the truth.

Clarissa shut her eyes tight, wishing away all her troubles, just as she had done when she was a child. Opening them again, she smiled when her gaze lit upon her reticule. She had not thought of those drawings since rolling them and placing them inside the small reticule. Now, she bounced off the bed and retrieved them, spreading them out carefully for a closer inspection.

Tristram's drawing of her and Monty

was enchanting. He had captured Monty's expression perfectly, and hers was quite accurate, too. She had no doubt that she had been gazing at him adoringly — before their misunderstanding. The other drawing made her lips curl in a wicked smile. She could never show it to anyone, but when she was feeling blue, she would always have this drawing to cheer her.

The door opened and the upstairs maid entered with a tray of chocolate.

"Good morning, Polly."

"Good morning, miss. Miss Bates thought you might like a cup of chocolate."

"How nice of her to think of me. Thank you for bringing it," she added. Not having her own maid, she was always pleasantly surprised and suitably grateful when the servants performed some kindness for her.

"It's another bright day, miss. Miss Landis is dressing to go for a drive. Miss Anderson thought you might wish to accompany her."

"Oh, yes, of course," said Clarissa. "Tell her I will be down in a trice."

The maid hurried away, and Clarissa drank her chocolate before dressing. She was ready in no time, choosing a modest carriage gown of dark green.

Glancing at the table by the bed, she

gasped. There lay Tristram's drawings. Frowning, she looked around her for someplace suitable to hide them. Her jewel case, the perfect place. She had no jewelry except her mother's pearls and those were only taken out for special occasions like the breakfast the day before. It was one place she could be certain Adele would never look since she had nothing worth borrowing.

First, however, she granted herself one final look. There, in the center, was the eight-legged Adele. On either side of her were Montgomery Darby and Lord Benchley, struggling against the deceptively strong web.

Oh, Tristram, you have captured her so well.

Putting the small jewelry case back in its drawer, she settled her bonnet on her head and hurried out the door.

Downstairs, she expected to find Adele waiting in the drawing room with Lord Benchley at her side. She was taken aback to discover Montgomery Darby there, looking more handsome than ever in his bottle green coat and shining Hessians. His smile widened when he saw her.

"Good afternoon, Miss Starnes," he said.

"Good afternoon," she returned, wishing there were some way she could gracefully back out of this intolerable situation. Adele watched her, smiling smugly.

"I . . . I invited your cousin to go for a drive this afternoon while we danced last night. I hope it is not an inconvenience for you to accompany us," he said.

"That is why Clarissa is here," said Adele. "When Miss Anderson is too fatigued, Clarissa is always here to take her place. Is that not right, Cousin?"

"Quite right, Adele," she agreed, pasting a smile on her face, determined that she would not allow her spoiled cousin to know how very devastated she was. She could not imagine a worse punishment than to be forced to watch Montgomery Darby pay court to her cousin.

"Excellent. I count myself twice blessed to be escorting two such beautiful ladies."

He offered each lady an arm, but Clarissa refused to notice and trailed after them, out the door, and down the steps to the marquess's waiting landaulet.

When Montgomery handed her up, Adele trilled, "Do sit in the rear-facing seat, Clarissa. I want dear Mr. Darby to sit here beside me."

"Certainly," she said coldly.

Monty was left with no choice but to take the place beside Adele. She hooked arms with him and sidled close while giving Clarissa a catlike smile.

"Mr. Darby is taking us to that charming little garden tearoom near Islington."

"Tristram is supposed to meet us there. He had an appointment this afternoon."

Clarissa again refused to meet his eyes. She could feel him staring at her, sending her silent messages. Well, she had not been born yesterday. She knew he was referring to Bow Street, but she would not give him the satisfaction of showing she cared.

"Are you familiar with the tearoom?" he asked finally.

"The one with the maze?" asked Clarissa. Good, she thought. She would be able to lose herself in the maze and not have to look at them together.

"Yes, though we don't want you spoiling it for us. Clarissa has the most manly sense of direction." Batting her lashes at Monty, Adele simpered, "I vow I cannot find my way out of the house. You will not mind being my personal guide, will you, Mr. Darby?"

"I would be delighted, Miss Landis," he replied, smiling down at her.

Clarissa wanted to slap both of them.

Whom was she deceiving, telling herself that his attentions might be switching from Adele to her? He was as besotted as ever. He might admire the way Clarissa had helped out in the crisis the previous night, but it had not blinded him to Adele's great beauty.

Now Adele seemed determined to have him, too, and she would not even be needed to make Adele jealous. Could things get any worse?

"Clarissa, please do not scowl at me like that," said Adele.

"Oh, was I scowling?" she asked sweetly. "I'm sure I have no reason to do so. The day is fine, and I am spending it with two of my favorite people. What more could I wish for?"

"Miss Landis, is that you?"

They turned to see Mr. Reed riding up to the carriage. As he stopped, his horse blocked the oncoming traffic, and soon the air was filled with shouting and curses.

"Might I join you?" asked the young man, completely oblivious to the hubbub he was causing.

"Of course you may, Mr. Reed. Poor Clarissa is pining away for an escort of her own," said Adele, all the while grinning at Clarissa.

"Meet us at the corner," commanded Montgomery, glaring at the young man. "You are holding up traffic."

"What? Oh, yes. Right away," he said, yanking back on the reins and upsetting his hired mount. The horse reared, and Mr. Reed ended up on the pavement, looking up at the sky.

In a smooth, nimble movement, Montgomery hopped to the ground and picked up the young man, grabbing his horse's reins and leading both of them back to the carriage.

"Get in," he commanded the dazed youth. He tied the hack to the back of the carriage and climbed inside, too.

Mr. Reed had taken Montgomery's seat, forcing him to sit beside Clarissa who was looking daggers at everyone.

"Mr. Reed gets faint when he rides backward. You do not mind, do you?"

"Of course not," he replied, his jaw working furiously.

"Miss Landis tells me we are going to a tearoom in the country. I had no idea they existed," said Mr. Reed, his sunny face defying anyone to crush his eagerness.

"Nor did I, but evidently they do," said Montgomery.

"I can tell you, Miss Landis, that I am

thoroughly enjoying myself here in London. Why, it has the most marvelous sights. And the people! Did I tell you that I spied the Prince Regent yesterday, simply riding through Hyde Park?"

"How thrilling for you," said Miss Landis.

"Yes, and I am beginning to get in the habit of knowing what stories I may repeat and which ones I should not. I would not, for instance, mention last night's debacle if I had not already heard it discussed and more at my club this morning."

"What debacle is that?" asked Montgomery.

Clarissa could feel the tension in the air, but Adele and Mr. Reed were oblivious to it.

"Why, that scandalous barge accident. Not that a barge is scandalous, or that the fireworks were. Rather, it was the people on that barge. I understand some of our best young men were on board last night. They sail along there regularly, I am told, having their wild org—"

"Be quiet, young man! Do you not realize that what you may hear at your club may not be at all suitable for young ladies to hear?" said Montgomery.

Mr. Reed colored up like a schoolgirl

and apologized profusely until Montgomery had to silence him once again — more gently, this time.

After what seemed an interminable interval, they arrived at the modest tearoom. The day being fine, they went straight through to the garden where several small tables and chairs had been set up. Another twenty paces away was the maze.

Though Adele had asked Montgomery to be her guide, she appeared to have lost interest in him since the addition of Mr. Reed to their party. For the most part, Clarissa and Montgomery listened in silence while the other two prattled on about what everyone had been wearing the previous night.

Finally, Montgomery rose and offered his arm to Clarissa, saying gruffly, "Would you care to go for a stroll, Miss Starnes?"

"Oh, no, Mr. Darby. You promised to lead me through the maze," whined Adele, jumping up and stepping between him and Clarissa. "Clarissa can go with Mr. Reed. We will enter here, and the two of you can go to the other side to enter."

"Miss Starnes?" said the young man, holding out his arm.

She forced a smile to her lips and took his arm.

"I am glad you are enjoying your stay, Mr. Reed," she said.

"Oh, yes. I say, Mr. Darby was being a bit rag mannered, don't you think? I mean, I know I cannot describe what went on, but to merely say the word orgy is not so bad, is it?"

She chuckled and said, "Mr. Reed, I assure you Mr. Darby was not being in the least stuffy. Ladies, such as my cousin and I, do not even wish to hear the word spoken."

"Really? Well, then I most humbly beg your pardon, Miss Starnes. I hope you know I would never wish to offend any lady."

"Yes, I believe you."

"Good. I mean, I thought Mr. Darby was being prudish because his brother was one of the men caught on that barge. I shouldn't doubt that his reaction was colored by that fact. I know that if my brother were at the center of such an outrageous scandal, I would not want it bruited about."

"Scandal?"

"Oh, yes. Some of the ladies are trying to ban the men who were on board from polite society."

"But they are just foolish young men."

"Perhaps, but some of the leaders of the *ton* do not see it like that, according to their husbands."

Clarissa dropped his arm, saying, "I should go and tell Monty at once." She turned and slammed against his broad chest.

"Monty!"

"Miss Starnes," he said, looking at Mr. Reed, who was shifting nervously from one foot to the other.

"Clarissa, how dare you call my suitor by his Christian name!" exclaimed Adele. "When I tell my mother . . ."

"I beg you will not, Miss Landis," said Montgomery, smiling into those clear blue eyes. "It may sound very discourteous, but I feel certain Miss Starnes is only in the habit of thinking of me and my brothers by our Christian names in order to keep us straight in her mind. I took no offense, Miss Starnes," he added.

"Very well," said Adele. "But you must learn to watch your tongue, Clarissa."

Clarissa's eyes flashed with anger, and she hurried away, following each twist and turn with unerring accuracy until she was out of the maze and back at the small table.

If she had thought he would follow her,

she was sadly mistaken. Instead, she could hear their laughter as the three of them continued on their way to the center of the maze. A tear trickled down her cheek, and she brushed it away angrily. She would will herself to care nothing for his opinion — or for him.

"Miss Starnes, how glad I am to have found you!" exclaimed Tristram, striding across the small lawn and taking her hand in his. "I must tell you about my appointment at Bow Street."

In answer, the indomitable Clarissa burst into tears.

Eight

"I say, Miss Starnes, whatever is the matter? What are you doing here all alone? Where is Monty?"

She only shook her head, and he put his arm around her, drawing her gently to him. After a moment, Clarissa lifted her head and managed to say between sobs, "Will you . . . take me . . . back to London?"

"Of course I shall. Let me just go and tell . . ."

"No! Can we not simply go? We can tell the landlord."

"Very well. Come along with me. Whatever has happened, I will not abandon you." Keeping a comforting arm around her shoulder, he led her through the tearoom and out the front door.

"It is a good thing I brought the barouche," he said, handing her into the empty carriage. "Will you be all right while I find the landlord and my driver?"

Nodding, she gave him a watery smile. When he was gone, Clarissa fished a tiny mirror out of her reticule and looked at herself. The mirror had been her mother's, and suddenly, she wished she could talk to her. The thought brought forth a fresh flood of tears. Even as she was telling herself how foolish it was to weep over her mother, who had been dead more than ten years, her sobbing grew louder.

The carriage dipped as Tristram and the driver climbed in. Looking at their faces, Clarissa was seized by a fit of the giggles. Truly alarmed now, the men looked ready to abandon ship. Clarissa bit her lip and managed to control her hysteria long enough for them to get under way.

After several minutes, when she had used Tristram's large handkerchief to mop her tears, Clarissa gave him a grateful smile, saying, "Thank you, Tristram, I mean, Mr. Darby." Really! She must curb this abominable tendency to think of the Darby brothers by their Christian names. That was what had gotten her into trouble in the first place.

But he was grinning and said, "You may call me Tristram, Miss Starnes. It is better than what Barton, our manservant calls me — Master Tristram. I feel like I am back in leading strings every time he says it. Still, it does simplify things, what with me, Max, and Monty all being Mr. Darby. Oh dear, what did I say?" he asked when fresh tears began to trickle down her cheeks.

Clarissa shook her head and refused to succumb to another bout of tears. Smiling, she said, "There. All better."

"Good," replied the nervous young man.

They rode in silence for a quarter of an hour. Clarissa could feel him stealing glances at her profile. She owed him an explanation, but she was uncertain that she could get through it without more tears.

And why was she crying? She had nothing to cry about. Montgomery Darby had never led her to believe he had the least interest in her, other than as a friend. She had made too much of his admiration the evening before. When it came down to it, he was set on wedding her cousin.

And she had agreed to help him, she thought, teetering on the brink of despair. But no, she would not allow it. Let him have Adele if he wanted her. She could never love a man who would settle for someone as self-centered as Adele.

Except that she did.

What of it? she demanded with ruthless candor. She would help him anyway. She would help him because she loved him, and he loved his — what was it called? Darwood Hall?

She grabbed Tristram's arm and his attention by exclaiming, "You are the one I wanted to talk to!"

"I am?" he said cautiously.

"Yes," she replied and then glanced at the driver. Looking around, she said, "Could we stop over there and go for a stroll?"

"Certainly. Nichols, pull up over by those trees. We wish to get down and stretch our legs."

When they had descended and were several yards away from the equipage, he asked, "What was that all about?"

"I apologize, Tristram, for commandeering you and your carriage like I did, but I suddenly found my cousin and . . . well, I found the situation intolerable."

"I am only happy that I arrived at an opportune time, Miss Starnes."

"You are very understanding. Here you have rescued me twice in the past two days, and without any questions."

"My pleasure. But tell me why we had to leave the carriage."

"Your driver is one of Lord Cravenwell's servants, is he not?"

"Yes. He sort of comes with the carriage. I do not drive, if I can help it, so I . . ."

"I understand, but I did not wish to

speak where we could be overheard."

"Good idea, though I am certain he will report all of this to his master. Still, we have nothing to hide. Now, what did you wish to talk about?"

"You will think me the veriest quiz, but I would so like to know about your brother's circumstances, about your family estate in Cornwall."

"About Darwood Hall? What on earth for? It is nothing but a pile of dusty beams and plaster. I find London much more agreeable."

"That is not what I mean. Oh, Tristram, I must ask you a most indelicate, improper question." They had been strolling all this time, but now, she stopped and turned to face him. "Is your brother looking out for an heiress because he is in danger of losing his home, the home he loves so dearly?"

Tristram grimaced and appeared to weigh his answer. "I do not think he is in danger of losing the Hall," he began cautiously.

"And if your father is thrown into debtor's prison?"

"Wherever did you get that notion?" he demanded.

"The Marquess of Cravenwell."

"The villain!" he said, walking away

from her for several paces before turning and staring at the carriage and driver. "So that is why you didn't wish to speak in the carriage."

"Yes, I feel certain your servants are reporting every word you speak to their true employer."

"Thank you, Miss Starnes. I will remember to watch my tongue. I do not care to think of servants spying on us. Was there something else you wished to say to me?" he asked, smiling at her.

"I . . . no, not really. I am afraid I acted rather foolishly back there. I apologize, and if you would care to return to the tearoom . . ."

"Not unless you want to. I just came out because Montgomery had invited me and I wanted to tell him how things went at Bow Street. Shall we continue back to town?"

"Yes, let's," said Clarissa, taking his arm and returning to the carriage.

She was glad he had not wanted to return to the tearoom. She would not have liked explaining her sudden departure. As it was, Adele would no doubt demand enlightenment, though for once in her life, she might not get what she wanted, thought Clarissa with a smile.

She closed her eyes, seeing Monty in her

216

mind's eye. He was still a good man, and she did not blame him for wanting to marry an heiress in order to keep his estate. It was done by other men all the time. If being deceptive about his financial state tarnished his image a little, who was she to throw stones? No, she had promised Monty that she would help him win Adele, and so she would — even if it broke her heart.

Setting aside her gloom, she asked, "What happened at Bow Street? Did you hire a runner?"

"Yes, I did, a Mr. Crumb. He said he should have something for me rather quickly. He didn't seem to think it would be difficult to locate the man."

"That is good. I hope you get your drawings back."

"So do I. There are one or two that Max and Monty would not want exposed," he said with a disarming grin. "Nothing scandalous, of course, since neither of them has been involved . . . well, there was last night's debacle with the pleasure barge, but I did not even attempt a drawing of that since Max was involved."

"So you are learning to be cautious. My chaperone, Miss Anderson, told me once that I should never put anything in writing that I did not want the world to know. Since your drawings are so accurate, I think you should apply the same rule to them," said Clarissa.

"I could not agree more. From now on, nothing but still lifes and animals."

Clarissa was completely composed by the time Montgomery Darby arrived home with her cousin. Knowing that Adele would be in a rage, she kept out of sight in the morning room, its door open so that she could hear what was said.

The front door opened, and she could tell immediately that Adele was trying to keep Monty from coming inside. He was being unusually determined, however, to thwart her efforts. Clarissa smiled. Adele knew she would not be able to keep her temper with Clarissa and did not wish to turn into a shrew in front of her suitor.

It was too tempting to resist, and Clarissa stepped into the hall, smiling brightly at the wrangling couple.

"Good afternoon, Mr. Darby, Adele."

Porter, she noted, took the precaution of shooing the footman out of the vicinity. Then he tried to melt into the wall in order to keep his first-rate view.

"Where did you go? And why?" exclaimed Adele, rushing forward and grabbing Clarissa's wrist.

"Go? But I thought Mr. Darby — Mr. Tristram Darby, that is, had left a note explaining all that. Did he forget to do so?"

"Not exactly," said Monty, who was watching her rather too closely. "The landlord merely told us you had taken ill, and I . . . We were worried about you."

"It was all a lie, just as I told you," said Adele. "Only look at her! She does not look in the least ill, does she?"

Monty smiled at this and said, "Not in the least."

"You are too kind, sir," Clarissa said, giving him her best impression of a flirt.

"Oh! Never mind that! Why did you leave, Clarissa? It was most rude of you!"

"Perhaps, but I did mention that I had the headache, and it became much worse, so when Mr. Tristram Darby arrived at the tearoom, I asked him to escort me home. I would not have done so if you had been left alone with Mr. Darby, Mr. Montgomery Darby, that is," she said, giving him another silly smile that served to enrage Adele even more.

Monty winked at her, grinning unabashedly. He was not a slow top, she thought. He knew she was trying to make Adele jealous, and his smile told her he was appreciative of her efforts.

Clarissa had never been so torn. Succeeding meant driving Adele into his arms. It also meant losing Monty.

"I still say it was horribly rude of you," said Adele.

"But we are glad you did not have to suffer, are we not, Miss Landis?" he asked.

Her lips pursed so tight, they were white, Adele agreed.

"Thank you for being so understanding," said Clarissa. "Now, I really must go upstairs. I feel my headache returning. If you will excuse me."

Adele glared at her, but Monty said, "Certainly, Miss Starnes. I hope you are soon feeling fit again."

"You are most kind," she said, turning and heading for the stairs, walking slowly so that she could catch the rest of their conversation.

"I should be going, Miss Landis. I have enjoyed this day with you more than I can say. I hope to see you at the Everson ball tomorrow night," he added, his voice eager as he bowed over her cousin's hand.

"I am looking forward to it, Mr. Darby," said Adele.

Clarissa cringed at her cousin's flat

tones. Poor Monty. It could mean only one thing. After an afternoon with him dancing attendance on her, Adele was feeling very sure of him, and that meant she would begin to lead him a merry dance.

Perhaps he will not care to follow, said a forlorn inner voice, raising its timid head for only a second before hiding in reality once again.

Clarissa was in no mood for dancing and frivolity, a terrible state to be in when one was attending a ball. She had watched every man make a cake of himself over her cousin, who was looking more radiant than ever in a pale rose silk gown, with a décolletage meant to tempt the strongest of men.

Monty, she discovered, much to her dismay, was not a strong man. He could not take his eyes off Adele or her creamy white breasts. For her part, Adele was pretending he was invisible. The tactic only seemed to enflame him.

Surely it could not last, thought Clarissa, sitting beside Miss Anderson. She had discovered that she could be invisible, too, if she sat among the chaperones and avoided looking at the gentlemen. Basking in

Adele's glow, they never saw beyond her sphere of light.

"Miss Adele is certainly in looks tonight," whispered Miss Anderson.

"When is she not?" grumbled Clarissa before remembering she was not alone. "I mean, my cousin is the prettiest young lady of the Season."

"Just like the last six," murmured Miss Anderson, her gray eyes lighting with mischief. Clarissa chuckled, and the chaperone added, "Not that she has lost her looks in any measure. I wonder, however, how much longer she can maintain them. You notice how she frowns so when she is displeased. I have tried to tell her that one of these days, that endearing little pouting frown will turn into a furrowed brow."

"Why, Miss Anderson, I do believe you are out of curl this evening. Has something happened to make you cross?"

The spinster shook her head. "No, I should not have spoken, but . . ."

"You may confide in me, Miss Anderson," said Clarissa.

"Very well. I must tell someone and since it involves you, it is only right that you should know."

"Go on," said Clarissa, her own brow puckered with concern.

"I overheard your aunt and uncle talking today, about Miss Adele and about you. About me, too, for that matter, but that is something I have been expecting for some time." Clarissa gave her a little nod of encouragement, and she continued. "After Miss Adele is wed, at the end of the Season, they plan to retire to the country. You are to go, too, and I will be dismissed."

"You are not telling me anything I hadn't already guessed, Miss Anderson. What will you do?"

"Do not worry about me. I have a mind to go to my sister. Her husband died last summer, and she needs my help. But it is you who concerns me, dear girl."

"I assure you, Miss Anderson, that I do not mind going to the country. On the contrary, I will be quite pleased to see the last of London for a while."

Miss Anderson dabbed at the tears that had sprung to her eyes. With a little sniff, she said, "For a long while, my dear. Your aunt and uncle plan to marry you off to the squire."

"The squire? Squire Perkins? I cannot credit it. His wife has been dead for only a year. He is hardly over that. And why should he wish to wed me?"

"You know he always had a soft spot for you, Miss Clarissa, and he has all those children to care for. They need a mother."

"They may need a mother, but they do not need me," she exclaimed, her voice rising so that people nearby turned to stare. Lowering her voice, Clarissa hissed, "I will not do it."

"But you have always been so friendly to him. Your aunt told your uncle that she felt certain you would be happy to have him. They think it is a good match."

"This is intolerable!" said Clarissa. "I must speak to Aunt Frances at once!" She rose, shaking off Miss Anderson's restraining hand.

Fuming, she made a beeline for her aunt, her pace slowing as she realized it would be impossible to extract her from her circle of friends. Glancing back at Miss Anderson, who had turned a pasty white, Clarissa's determination wavered. Coming to a halt by a column, she stopped, shaking her head and muttering to herself. If she asked her aunt about what was said, her aunt would be very angry with Miss Anderson. She might even discharge her immediately.

"That is the first sign of madness, they say."

Clarissa looked into those dark brown eyes and gave him a pathetic smile.

Monty frowned and took her elbow, leading her behind the column and out of sight of curious onlookers. "Whatever is the matter, Miss Starnes?"

"I . . . I cannot say. It is of a private nature," she said, willing him to probe further. How wonderful it would be to unburden herself to him. And if he should offer to rescue her from her predicament? But no, she could not allow that.

"Then I shall not pry, but I hope you know that you may rely on me, even if you should find yourself in the direst of straits."

Looking into that sincere face, she could not doubt he would save her if he could. Unfortunately, he needed saving himself — or his beloved Darwood Hall did. Why did everything have to be so very complicated?

Smiling, she said, "You are very kind, Mr. Darby. I shall come about, have no fear of that."

"I feel certain you will, Miss Starnes. You are a most extraordinary young lady. Now, do you perhaps have a dance left for me?"

"Yes," she said, suddenly feeling much better. It was amazing what spending a few moments with him could do for her spirits. "As a matter of fact, I have all of them free. I have not felt like dancing tonight . . . until now."

"Well then, I shall claim the one just starting, and we shall quickly fill the rest of your evening once the gentlemen realize you are available."

"You and your brothers cannot dance with me all night," she said.

"No, no. Besides, only Tristram accompanied me tonight."

"Oh, I am sorry. I was looking forward to seeing your brother Max again."

"And once again, he is too busy with his new friends to have time for polite society. But Tris is here, and he will be delighted that you have spared a dance for him. But first, my dance."

"Really, Monty, you do not have to dance with me. I know you would much rather be with Adele."

"Nonsense," he said, his tone bracing. Then, more subdued, he added, "At any rate, I do not seem to be in favor tonight so I will leave the field to Benchley. He is welcome to her." He took her in his arms and swept her onto the dance floor for the waltz.

"You mustn't be too upset with Adele.

She has always gotten her way, you know," said Clarissa.

"I understand that," he said. "What I cannot understand is how she can think I do not love her."

"She said that?"

"She intimated as much when she was telling everyone about our outing to the tearoom," he said, forcing a feeble smile.

"But she enjoyed herself immensely. She told me so."

"And so I thought, but she has been very cool to me all evening."

"I am sorry, Monty," said Clarissa, squeezing his hand to offer him comfort.

"If I knew what she wanted from me, I would not hesitate to perform any service for her."

"I know," said Clarissa, thinking privately that what her cousin needed was to be spanked like a spoiled child, but it would never do to tell Monty that. Instead, she said, "I have it! Tomorrow night, we are to attend Mrs. Andrew's card party. Are you very good at cards?"

"Barely competent," he replied, but his manner was more hopeful than before.

"It makes no difference. Adele cannot abide losing at anything, even cards. You must play against her and lose."

"On purpose?"

"No, not on purpose. You are, by your own words, a wretched player. You will not need to pretend, and she will be happy to have won and will want to console you," said Clarissa. Some might call it gloating, but Adele did not see it that way.

"I will try it," he said, smiling down at her. "Playing the attentive lover is not proving advantageous."

They made several circuits around the ballroom before he spoke to her again. Clarissa drank in the sound of his voice, forgetting that the words were sealing her doom.

"I really do not know how to thank you, Clarissa. You have been so kind, advising me on courting your cousin. You are an extraordinary young lady. I only wish there were something I could do to repay you."

She smiled up at him, storing up the tone of his voice, the words of praise, and saving them for memories in the bleak future.

"It is my pleasure to help you, Monty," she replied. "That is all the reward I need."

Monty was true to his word, although it took him some time to scour the house before finding Tristram and returning him to the ballroom where he claimed her hand.

It was the waltz, too, and she was thoroughly amused by his comments about the other guests as they progressed around the floor.

"You see those two ladies?" he whispered.

"Yes, Mrs. Davenport and Lady Nugent."

"Earlier, they each had a hold of that young fellow over there, tugging him in opposite directions as they tried to secure him for their daughters. Those ostrich plumes in their turbans waved back and forth, nearly blinding the poor fellow."

Clarissa laughed and laughed, and when their waltz was done, she said, "You should write down your observations, Tristram. You are as talented with words as you are with drawings."

"How nice of you to say so, Clarissa," he said, calling her by her first name as if she were his sister. "I do write them down."

Lowering his voice, he said confidentially, "I am writing a novel. The hero of the piece is Sir Milton, modeled, as you might guess, on my brother Max."

"How exciting. I hope you will allow me to read it someday."

"Perhaps," he said, blushing to the roots of his blond hair. "I am not certain it is good enough to share, but I do enjoy writing it."

"Perhaps you will include me in it," she teased.

"Perhaps I will. I have included your cousin in a small role."

"Have you?"

"Oh, yes. Every novel needs a villainess," he said, winking at her as the music came to an end.

Clarissa spent the rest of the evening being handed from one partner to the next. She did not precisely enjoy herself, for she was too upset about her aunt and uncle's plans for her to feel carefree. But she did manage to converse rationally and behave normally.

Tristram's resolution to refrain from drawing anything controversial was short-lived. The next day, armed with the publisher's address from the Bow Street Runner, he confronted the man who had bought one of his drawings from the thief.

"Good morning," he said cheerily as he entered the dirty, noisy shop.

"I don't have any money to buy anything," said the plump, middle-aged man, wiping his hands on his apron.

"I haven't said I was selling anything,"

replied Tristram. "I want some information." He placed the broadsheet of Lord Grant and his high shirt points on the counter. "Where did you get this?"

The man glanced at it and shook his head. "Bought it off a fellow. I wanted to buy more, but he only sold me the one. What do you care? It's not you in the drawing," he added, looking Tristram up and down.

"No, but it is my drawing, and it was stolen from me less than a week ago."

"Well, I had no way of knowing that, now, did I? I've only your word on it."

Tristram grabbed a piece of crumpled paper off the floor, smoothed it out and applied his pencil to it, rendering an almost perfect copy of the broadside.

"There, now do you believe me?"

The man stroked his chin until a little smile curved his thick lips. "You are obviously a swell, a man of the upper crust. What would you say if I offered you a shilling for more drawings like this?"

"A shilling? You must be joking," said Tristram.

"Two shillings?"

"No less than a guinea each."

"That's highway robbery, it is!"

"Yes, but your original offer was nothing

more than robbing me."

"Only on one condition, young fellow. I put out this paper twice each week. I want a drawing for each edition."

"I could do that. When do you want the first one?" asked Tristram.

"Five minutes ago, Mr. . . . ?"

"Tr . . . Tom Smith," he replied, offering his hand to shake.

"Pleased to meet you, Mr. Smith. And I'm Cain, just Cain. No Mister."

"Happy to make your acquaintance. Now, if you have a clean sheet of paper, I will produce a drawing for your news-paper."

Tristram sat down on a tall stool and bent over the paper, making certain that the faces of the two matrons with massive bosoms and huge turbans resembled no one of his acquaintance. In between them, an elegantly dressed buck with money peeking out of his pockets, was being used like the rope in a very nasty tug of war.

Handing it to Cain, Tristram said, "I don't think this one will need a caption."

Montgomery managed to drag Max along to Mrs. Andrew's card party the next evening. Max was an expert at cards, though he never wagered more than a penny or two. He had inherited their father's love of gaming without the need to lose his shirt. Max had been informed that he was to partner Adele in their game of whist, thereby insuring that she would be a happy winner.

Pulling him to one side before play began, Clarissa asked, "Are you prepared to lose handsomely?"

"Not only am I prepared," he said. "But I have brought my brother who is not only skilled, but lucky, too. Max cannot possibly lose, and he has agreed to partner your cousin."

"Wonderful. Do you think you and I might . . . ?"

"Of course," he said. "You must be my partner since you are in on the plan! That will make it perfect!"

Fifteen minutes later, the four of them were seated at a table, cards dealt, and the queen of hearts facing up to mark the trump suit.

An hour later, the first rubber had been completed. Adele was grinding her teeth, Monty was appalled, and Max and Clarissa could not contain their amusement.

"What are you two giggling about?" snapped Adele.

"Nothing, Adele," said Clarissa.

Adele pushed away from the table, and the Darby brothers leapt to their feet. "I will be back in a few minutes, and we will play another rubber," she announced.

"Devil take me! That is one angry female," whispered Max, grinning at his brother and Clarissa.

"Oh, dear. I should not have laughed," said Clarissa.

"No, you should not!" agreed Monty. "What has gone wrong? Max, you never lose."

"Occasionally, even I am out of luck, and tonight is one of those nights. I have tried my best, Monty, but the cards are not cooperating — neither for Miss Landis nor for me."

"And I cannot lose," said Clarissa. "Every hand, I have almost all the trumps. I am sorry, Monty, but there was nothing I could do."

"I know, I know. I think the gods are conspiring against me."

"Perhaps you will be able to comfort her, old fellow," said Max.

"It is hardly likely that Miss Landis will want comfort from her opponent," he said dryly, standing up again as Adele returned to the table.

They played another rubber and things were much the same. Even Adele could not blame her partner for the defeat since both of them were dealt one horrible hand after another. By the end, she was smiling and laughing, too.

Monty cannot keep his eyes off her, thought Clarissa miserably. Despite her plans going awry, the evening had turned out just as Monty had hoped — Adele was once again smiling on him.

Mrs. Andrew, a formidable matron, announced supper at midnight. Afterward, she commanded that everyone had to switch games and partners, so Clarissa parted from Monty.

When they were leaving, he pulled her to one side and whispered, "Do you go to the Davenport masked ball tomorrow night?"

"We will be there," she replied.

"What is Adele to wear?"

"I really do not know. She is keeping it a secret. Perhaps if you call tomorrow, she will tell you."

"What are you two whispering about?" asked Adele, gliding up to Monty and putting her hand on his arm.

"I was asking what you are wearing to the Davenport masquerade ball tomorrow night," he replied.

"Naughty boy," purred Adele. "It was to be a surprise, but I shall tell you."

Clarissa shrugged, and moved away. She could not bear to watch as Adele whispered in Monty's ear.

He shook his head and said, "I cannot wear that, Miss Landis. I wouldn't know where to find such a costume."

"If you wish to escort me into supper, gallant knight, you will find one." With a giggle, Adele left his side.

While Montgomery Darby was allowing Barton to put the finishing touches on his costume that evening, his brothers were watching with interest.

"Shouldn't you wait to put on the gloves until everything else is done?" asked Max.

"How should I know," grumbled Montgomery.

"Have you seen the latest, Monty," said Tristram, holding out the scandal sheet that had his drawing plastered across the back of it.

"Good grief, Tristram. I told you not to draw people we know," said Montgomery.

"Well, I did not draw anyone in particular," he said, frowning down at the paper. "I was very sure of that."

"Perhaps you did not mean to do so, but

everyone at the ball the other night will remember who was using this poor fellow as a rope in their tug of war. Mrs. Davenport and Lady Nugent had the young man practically crying for an escape."

"I never thought anyone would remember that," mumbled Tristram.

"I know; just try to be even more careful. We cannot afford to anger Society should anyone discover who is drawing these pictures. The fact that the drawing is of something that took place at a ball is enough to tell everyone that the artist is a member of their own set. We just cannot afford the scandal."

"You're right, Monty. I will do better."

"Good, now how do I look?" asked Monty after Barton had secured his helmet on his head.

"You look like a fool," said Max, eyeing his brother and shaking his head.

"I feel like a fool," said Monty, clanking as he turned to see himself in the glass.

"I think you look very authentic," said Tristram. "Sometimes, it helps to have servants that overhear things," he added, looking pointedly at Barton.

Barton turned pink and scuttled out of the room.

"You shouldn't tease him like that," said

Monty. "Especially since he went to the marquess and borrowed this suit of mail. I wish it were not quite so heavy."

"Oh, quit worrying," said Max. "You'll do fine."

"I suppose. But it would have been easier to wear a domino."

With a swirl of their capes, Max and Tristram put on their dominoes and picked up their masks.

"Lead on, good knight. You can slay any dragons we meet along the way," said Max.

"There's only one that needs slaying," muttered Tristram, his words drowned out by the clanking of Montgomery's suit of armor.

Nine

The Davenports had money, and they had spared no expense in planning their masked ball. For Mrs. Davenport, who was doing all she could to get the first of five daughters settled, it was an investment.

The ballroom was a sea of silver and navy blue silk. It hung from the ceiling and along the walls. The huge ballroom was open to the supper room where a sumptuous buffet waited, its offering continuously renewed by the army of footmen. In the center of the table was a four-foot ice sculpture of Neptune.

The gardens, too, had been dressed for the occasion. More blue and silver silk billowed over the terrace balcony, and colored lanterns dotted the pathways. A wooden dance floor had been constructed at the bottom of the terrace steps, and the musicians had been placed by the open doors so that the music floated outside, allowing couples to dance both in and out of doors.

Clarissa only half-listened to Adele as she chattered excitedly all the way to the ball. Adele wore the green silk and velvet gown of a medieval lady, with a cone-shaped hat that had several lengths of gauzy silk protruding from the top. She looked quite lovely, as usual.

Clarissa had chosen to dress as a shepherdess, though she had left her staff at home. She disliked masked balls, but not for the right reason. Miss Anderson condemned them for the rather loose behavior they encouraged. Clarissa disliked them because she preferred to know with whom she was dancing. Tonight, she planned to stay close to Miss Anderson and thus avoid the unknown.

Clarissa, however, had not counted on Adele's notion of amusement. It was apparent, however, soon after their arrival. Adele refused to wear a half mask, preferring to carry her mask on a stick and put it up to her face only for its flirtatious effect. Within minutes of their arrival, she had her usual cluster of admirers vying for a dance. Every man was dressed in various stages of armor, though none wore the full suit.

Clarissa could not resist commenting, "I thought you were keeping your costume a secret, Adele."

"And so I did," she simpered, smiling at each of the men in turn. "Except from my favorite beaux."

Just then, another knight approached her, dressed in full armor, including the helmet, with its visor down. After treading on the toes of Mr. Pitchly and Lord Grant, the knight said something undistinguishable.

"I beg your pardon, good knight, but I cannot understand you. Do, please, raise your visor," said Adele.

With Clarissa's help, the knight did so. Panting from the effort, Monty said, "Good evening, fair damsel."

Adele giggled and replied, "Good heavens, Mr. Darby, however do you expect to dance with me? I'm sure I never thought you would go so far."

"But your wish is my command, dear lady," he replied.

"So I see," she said, smiling smugly.

"Miss Landis, they are striking up a waltz. Shall we?" asked Mr. Pitchly, holding out his arm.

With a mocking smile for Monty, Adele tripped off to the dance floor. Her other admirers drifted away to watch, leaving Clarissa and Monty alone.

"I think you look magnificent," she said.

"I look like a metal-plated looby," he said, looking about him and leaning his ax against the wall. "I thought she wanted me to . . . oh, never mind. Would you care to, uh, sit with me?"

"I would deem it a privilege," she replied, taking his arm. "Let us go outside and find a quiet spot. The ball is barely underway, and already it is a sad crush. Mrs. Davenport will be in high gig."

"Perhaps she will find someone to take that daughter off her hands," he whispered when they had reached the terrace.

"Miss Davenport is a very pretty girl," said Clarissa.

"Yes, yes," he replied, waiting while she sat down on a stone bench. "Miss Davenport is a very pretty girl, but her voice positively grates on one's ears. Perhaps, when she is a little older, she will not sound quite so much like a squealing piglet."

"It is not very kind of you to point it out, Monty. The child cannot help it if her voice is high-pitched," said Clarissa, giving him a reproving frown.

"Oh, forgive me, Miss Starnes. It is this costume. I feel out of sorts and very foolish in it. I only hope I can make it through the evening without disgracing myself," said Monty. Sitting down beside Clarissa, he groaned, "Oh, this is rather cold when wearing armor."

Clarissa giggled and smiled up at him.

"Would you like me to help you remove your helmet?"

"Yes, thank you. There are a couple of fasteners right . . . there," he said, sighing with relief when she lifted it off the top of his head. He placed it on the flagstone and said, "Thank you, Miss Starnes. Once again, you have come to my rescue."

"It is always a pleasure, Mr. Darby," she said, switching to the more formal mode of address as other couples wandered onto the terrace.

"You are looking quite lovely tonight, if I may say so."

"You certainly may, and I thank you for the compliment. I fear I am not very original, but the gown is very comfortable."

"And the color suits you. I have noticed that when you wear deep yellows, your eyes are quite golden in color."

"Really? I have never noticed. My eyes are usually so lifeless," she said.

"Lifeless? I would never have described them in that manner," he replied. "You have very expressive eyes."

"There you are!" said Adele, dropping Mr. Pitchly's arm and glaring down at them. "I thought you said you wished to dance with me tonight, Mr. Darby."

Monty clambered to his feet to face her,

saying, "And so I did, Miss Landis, but that was before I showed up dressed in full armor. I had not considered that it would be impossible to dance while wearing all this."

"Still, if you truly wanted to dance, you could do so," she said, sticking out her bottom lip in a childish pout.

"Really, Miss Landis, you cannot wish to dance with me. As much as I long to do so, I would not dream of it. I might step on your toe and break it," he added with a little laugh.

Adele, however, would have none of it. Stamping her foot, she said, "You will dance with me, Mr. Darby."

"Miss Landis, surely you do not wish to dance with me tonight."

"Oh, but I do, Mr. Darby," she said, a tear trickling down her cheek.

It was too much for Monty, and he gave her a creaky bow and said, "For you, I shall do my best. If you will excuse me, Miss Starnes."

"Certainly," she replied, rising and disappearing into the ballroom. Mr. Pitchly shrugged his shoulders and followed.

"It is the quadrille," said Adele. "But we will pretend it is the waltz."

"Very well," he said. Montgomery removed his gauntlets and placed them on top of his helmet before taking Miss Landis's hand and leading her to the center of the terrace.

It was awkward, trying to waltz to a melody that was written in quadruple time. His movements were stiff and noisy. Even the breeze undermined his efforts as it ruffled the wispy silk scarves that trailed from Adele's tall headdress and blew them in his face. Monty released her hand to remove them, but they were caught fast on the fine mesh of his mail armor.

"I beg your pardon, Miss Landis. I fear you are not enjoying this dance very much."

"Just be careful. You have caught my dress in your armor, too," she said, shaking her arm to loosen the fine fabric. She favored him with a dazzling smile, and Montgomery redoubled his efforts, but her scarves kept blinding him.

"Miss Landis, I . . . this is not going well," he said.

"Nonsense, you are doing fine. And look, we are attracting an audience," she added with a giggle.

Montgomery looked up and groaned. The terrace was filling with people, jostling each other for a better view.

"Haven't they anything better to do?" he grumbled, forgetting to watch his feet and treading on the tip of her toe.

"Ouch!" she yelped, and he tried to back away.

Jumping back, Montgomery lost his balance, tumbling down the terrace steps and taking Miss Landis with him, though he did his best to protect her. They ended on the lawn with him sprawled on top of her. He rolled off immediately and sat up.

"Arghh!" she screamed, flailing against his breast-plate, hurting her hands and howling more loudly still. "Get away from me, you oaf!"

"But Miss Landis, you asked me to dance with you!"

Laughter erupted from their audience, and she kicked him with all her might. Tears, more wailing, and insults spewed forth as she hopped up and down, holding her injured foot.

"Miss Landis," said Montgomery, reaching for her, but Adele pushed him away, lost her balance and landed on the damp grass once again.

Rising with as much dignity as she could, she screamed, "You bumbling cretin!"

Montgomery held out her ruined headdress, and she took it, throwing it back in his face. Spinning about, she slogged her way up the terrace steps and into the house. Only Mr. Reed and Lord Grant stepped forward to accompany her. The other onlookers began to discuss the delicious tale and laugh all the louder.

Montgomery managed to get on his feet while the guests recovered from their merriment. Calls of sympathy and ridicule accompanied this movement until finally, all was quiet, and he was alone.

"Damn," he muttered, walking toward the stone steps.

Clarissa hurried down the steps and put her hands on his arms, exclaiming, "Good heavens, Monty. Are you all right? You did not injure yourself, did you?" As she spoke, she picked blades of grass off his breastplate. "I only heard the tale."

"Just bruised, in more ways than physically," he said with a rueful grin.

"Pay no heed to those people. They are not important. And Adele will recover, too," she murmured, standing on tiptoe to smooth his ruffled hair.

Moonlight and madness, she thought fleetingly as she gazed into his dark eyes. His lips were so close to hers. A gentle touch, and his lips met hers for one sweet, heart-stopping moment.

Backing away, Clarissa's hand flew to her mouth. With a shake of her head, she was gone, following in her cousin's footsteps and into the house.

Once inside the Davenports' ballroom, Clarissa felt a strong arm close around her shoulder. She looked up to find Tristram's kind gaze on her. Behind him, Max was watching her, too. The sympathy she read there told her that they had seen everything, and tears sprang to her eyes.

"Shh," whispered Tristram, taking her hand and following Max, away from the rest of the crowd, past the front doors and down the hall until they had discovered an empty room. Pulling her inside, Tristram held her until she stopped shaking.

"I . . . I cannot believe . . ." she began, her teeth chattering.

"Do not think of it. It was nothing," he whispered while leading her to a pair of chairs near the fire.

Sitting down opposite her, Tristram patted her hand. Max turned his attention to the fire, stirring the embers and giving her time to recover.

"You are right. It was nothing," whispered Clarissa.

"Does Monty know that you are in love

with him?" asked Max, startling both Clarissa and Tristram.

"Of course not. I would not dare to tell him. First of all, he would probably laugh in my face," she said, unable to meet her listeners' eyes as she spoke the lie.

"Clarissa, you know that is not true," said Tristram.

"Oh, very well. Monty would not laugh, but he might be swayed, and he mustn't be. He has to think of Darwood Hall. It is all he has ever wanted."

"Is it? Perhaps you are right, up to now. But I think you are selling our brother short," said Max.

"Have you never noticed the way he looks at Adele? He is so in love with her, he cannot see anything else. In his eyes, she is perfection itself," added Clarissa miserably.

"Then he is blind as well as daft," said Tristram. "What I do not understand, is why you have been helping him court your cousin. That makes no sense."

"I know it sounds silly," said Clarissa, her eyes softening and her lips curving into a sweet smile. "But when you love someone, you want to make them happy. For your brother, that means saving Darwood Hall."

"But Clarissa, it is only an estate. You are more important than that!" said the passionate Tristram.

"Not to your brother. Besides, we are forgetting that he loves Adele, not me."

"Does he?" said Tristram, holding out his hand and helping her rise. "Even Max, who is not very perceptive about such matters, thinks there is something between you."

"You are dears to tell me this," said Clarissa, smiling at the two brothers with sweet melancholy. "And truly, I wish it were so, but I cannot believe it."

"Then there is nothing left to say," said Max.

Tristram rose and held out his hand, "Come along. You have been moping long enough. Will you do me the honor of the next dance, Miss Starnes?"

They returned to the ballroom and were immediately accosted by Adele, visibly upset, her lower lip trembling. Other than this and the lack of her headdress, there was no sign that she had suffered any mishap. She was as lovely as ever.

"Clarissa, we must leave immediately," she hissed. "Miss Anderson is calling for the carriage."

"Whatever is the matter?" asked Clarissa.

"I . . . I cannot discuss it here," she replied, shaking her head vehemently.

"Shall I stay?" Tristram asked Clarissa.

"No, go away, you silly boy," said Adele.

Tristram waited until Clarissa had given him a nod.

"I will be fine," she said quietly. "Thank you for . . . for everything."

As he walked away, Adele growled, "I will not have you associating with any member of the Darby family!"

"*You* will not? Adele, I take leave to tell you that I will speak to anyone I please."

At this, the usually self-assured Miss Landis burst into tears. Clarissa quickly led her to the front door where Miss Anderson ushered them into their waiting carriage.

"How was the masked ball?" asked Barton, leaping out of the easy chair and setting aside his glass.

Tristram frowned, but Montgomery moaned, "Oh, what the deuce difference does it make. He'll find out everything anyway. Come over here and help me out of this demmed armor, Barton, while Tristram tells the tale. He is near to bursting as it is."

"It will be the scandal of the Season!" exclaimed Tristram, bounding across the room and perching on the arm of the sofa where Max was lounging. "Miss Landis was at her best. She was an absolute virago!"

"Do you mind, halfling?" said Montgomery, whose eyes were twinkling despite his words. "You happen to be speaking of the woman I hoped to marry. Ouch! Careful, Barton."

"Never mind him, Tris," said Max. "Go on with your tale."

"There were all of her swains, dressed alike, like good little puppies, and there she is, in the middle, like a queen bee. Monty, here, is dressed in full armor, but the others had enough sense not to do so. Perhaps she has done this before."

"Those happen to be my ears, Barton," grumbled Montgomery as the servant pulled the mail cowl over his head.

"So sorry, Master Montgomery," said Barton, all the while watching Tristram's animated face.

"Then she decides that Monty must dance with her — the waltz, nothing else would do — and of course, it was a disaster!"

The servant could not resist exclaiming, "She expected him to dance? In a full suit of armor?"

"It gets better," said Max, sparing a

glance for his twin, who had been divested of his armor and now sat in a soft chair, holding out his hand for the large drink Barton was pouring.

"So they are on the terrace, and she has these . . . things flying all about."

"They were scarves on her medieval headdress," supplied Monty.

"Yes, well, they kept getting tangled in Monty's mail suit, and finally, he stepped on her toe."

"I did not," protested Monty. Chuckling, he added, "It was the merest tip of her shoe."

"Whatever it might have been, it was enough for her to push him away, and over he went, tumbling down the terrace steps with her rolling right down to the bottom with him, kicking and screaming all the way!" said Tristram.

"What happened next?" asked Barton, caught up in the tale. He blushed, but the brothers paid no heed to this.

"She scrambled to her feet, still hitting him, and then she kicks him, but on his breastplate, so then she is yelling about that hurting so much. Finally, two of her other followers come and get her, and she is screaming like a fishmonger's wife all the way."

"She was not cursing," said Max.

"Certainly not," said Monty. "I really could not understand what she was saying."

"A good thing, too, since none of it was complimentary," said Tristram. "I tell you, it was better than any of the plays we will ever hope to see."

"I am so happy I could afford you a bit of entertainment," came Monty's dry comment.

"Well, you did, in more ways than one," said Tristram with a sly grin. "After Miss Landis had gone, then . . ."

"Tristram, that is enough," snapped Montgomery, rising and glaring at his little brother.

"But Monty . . ."

"No, do not say another word."

Tristram looked decidedly mulish for a moment, but then he smiled, took out his sketchbook, saying, "Very well, Monty. I'll not say another word."

"What else happened?" asked Barton. "If you don't mind my asking, sir."

"Nothing. Nothing at all," said Monty. "I am going to bed. Barton, do not wake me at all tomorrow. Perhaps by the following day, I will be ready to face the world again."

"Very good, Mr. Darby."

"Good night, sweet knight," said Tristram with a chuckle.

"Shaddup," came the only reply.

Monty went to his room and sat down on the edge of the bed to remove his dancing shoes. It had been a waste of time to wear them under his armor, he thought dismally.

It was not that he minded so very much making a fool of himself. Nor did he feel responsible for Miss Landis's foolish outburst. Had it not been she who insisted they dance?

No, it was the small, insignificant kiss that he had received from Miss Starnes. Clarissa. A small insignificant kiss whose sweetness and promise had brought him to his knees. Figuratively speaking, of course.

It was not that this small action had made him cease loving Miss Landis. No, he was not so fickle as that. Rather, it made him wonder why, if he loved Miss Landis as much as he thought he did, why Clarissa's kiss had affected him in the least.

It was a puzzle, he thought, yawning and stretching as he stood and crawled into bed. But it was not puzzling enough to make him stay awake another minute, and he slept.

There were only two bouquets of flowers on the table in the hall when Clarissa went downstairs the next morning, an unusual happening after her cousin had attended a ball of any sort. She was about to pass them by when Porter stopped her, presenting her with a silver tray that contained a gilt-edged envelope.

"What is this?"

"It arrived for you this morning, miss, with that bouquet of flowers."

"How delightful," she said, opening the card, her eyes widening as she read the note from Tristram Darby. "It is from Mr. Tristram Darby. He is such a kind young man," she said.

"Not so very young, miss," said the butler.

"Perhaps not, but younger than I am."

"By a few months, perhaps," said the butler, tidying the invitations that lay on the table.

Clarissa entered the breakfast room in a thoughtful mood. She shook her head, unwilling to believe that Tristram's words of admiration signified anything other than friendship.

As she nibbled on her toast, she toyed with the idea, and finally dismissed it as pure rubbish. Tristram was her friend, nothing more, and that suited both of them. Besides, he knew about her feelings for his brother. Even if he did have a certain warmth of feeling for her, he knew she could not return it.

"Good morning, Clarissa," said her uncle as he entered the room.

"Good morning, Uncle Clarence. It is a lovely morning. Would you care to go for a ride in the park with me?"

He heaved a sigh and said, "I think that might be a very good thing to do, my dear. I fear I am feeling a bit blue-deviled."

"What has upset you, if you do not mind telling me?"

"Oh, it is the usual. I am worried about Adele, forever worried about Adele. I cannot believe that she has not settled on one suitor. I really thought this younger man, this Mr. Darby, was going to win her, but now it appears she is disenchanted with him. I begin to wonder if she will ever choose a husband."

"I am sure Adele will know when it is time, Uncle," said Clarissa.

"I would say it is past time," he said, stuffing a slice of bacon into his mouth. "Perhaps I have been too patient. I thought Adele knew her own mind. She has always been headstrong," he added with a little chuckle.

"Yes, Uncle, and you know that you love that about her," said Clarissa, smiling at him. In her mind, she wanted to ask him if he might be as lenient with her when she refused to wed the squire back home. She rather thought all of his patience would be used up by the time Adele had decided to wed Monty.

"Nevertheless, I am going to tell her that she must make a choice before the end of the month. I cannot stand any more of this maddening mull."

Clarissa finished her toast and took a sip of tea before rising. "Shall I send for your horse, too, Uncle Clarence?"

"What? No, no, I am not in the mood for riding anymore. You run along without me. Do remember to take the groom, my dear."

"Certainly I will," she said, placing a kiss on the top of his head as she passed.

It was already ten o'clock, and her groom rode in front, clearing the way for his mistress as they progressed toward Green Park.

"Out o' me way, you blackguard," he shouted, raising his hand when the fruit seller's cart was not moved quickly enough.

"I am in no hurry, Mitch," protested Clarissa.

"Doesn't matter, miss. The likes o' him ain't got any right t' block the likes o' you," said the groom, continuing to bully his way through the streets until they had reached the quiet of the park.

"Thank you, Mitch," she said, riding ahead of him.

"Yer welcome, miss. Just remember, I cannot keep up with that mare o' yours."

"I shall remember."

"It's later than usual, too, you know," added the bossy groom. "More people about."

"Yes, I can see that," Clarissa called, giving the mare a little kick that sent her cantering down the path.

She had just reached the trees when a huge black stallion appeared, galloping as if the devil himself were after him. It was not the devil, but a red roan in hot pursuit, and Clarissa's usually docile mare had had quite enough. Snowdrop reared up on her hind legs and danced for a moment before coming down with bone-jarring force.

"Ouch!" cried Clarissa, tasting blood as she bit her tongue.

"Oh, upon my honor!" she mumbled, running her swollen tongue across her lips.

Her groom appeared. Out of breath and out of patience, he cried, "Blast his eyes! Oh, beg pardon, miss. I saw everything. Are you all right?"

"I hab bidden my tongue," she said, holding her handkerchief to her mouth.

"It's not bleedin'," said Mitch, looking at the still-snowy cloth.

"No thanks to that maniac," she said, wincing again.

Suddenly, they heard the pounding hooves, though slower this time. Clarissa took a firm hold on the reins, relaxing when she recognized Maxwell Darby. He was grinning from ear to ear, though her expression soon wiped the smile from his face.

"Terribly sorry, Miss Starnes. Didn't mean to startle you."

"It was my horse you startled, Max," she said, "and I have the swollen tongue to prove it."

"Really? Oh, I am sorry. I didn't realize the difference a couple of hours would make. Still, after the ball last night, I could not bring myself to rise any earlier. How are you feeling this morning, Miss Starnes?" he asked, swinging the big stallion around and riding alongside her.

Grumbling under his breath, her groom followed after them.

"I am fine, but what did you mean before, Mr. Darby? What have you been doing?" she asked, glancing at the big horse's foam-flecked neck.

"Just making a bit o' money on the side," he said, grinning down at her.

"How?" she asked, frowning at him when he hesitated. "The least you can do is tell me why I was run down in the middle of the park."

"Oh, very well," he said, his smile returning. "I race here in the mornings."

"Race? Here?" she asked as he nodded to each query. "Every morning?"

"Not every morning, perhaps, but several times each week."

"But I understood that you had no money."

"Nor did I until I won my first race. Let Monty go home with a wealthy bride. I have found a way to make money without saddling myself with a wife."

"I cannot believe what I am hearing," she breathed. "Were you not afraid of losing?"

"Couldn't lose," he said, patting his horse's neck. "Not with Thunderlight."

"But how would you have paid if you had lost?"

"But I was in no danger of losing. If

there is one lesson I have learned from my father, it is to wager only on a sure thing, and Thunderlight is a sure thing."

"But surely, Mr. Darby, you had to put up some sort of money."

"No, we race for horses. I win the other fellow's horse. I sell them — usually back to the same fellow — and then I have money in my pocket. It is as simple as can be."

Clarissa opened her mouth to protest, to lecture him, but he was smiling down at her with that same endearing expression his twin used, and she simply did not have the heart.

His blue eyes dancing, he added for good measure, "If I should stay here in London through the entire Season, I calculate that I can not only turn my land into a real farm, I should have enough to build a house, too."

"So that you can have a place to take this bride you say you do not want," teased Clarissa.

Max frowned and then laughed. He said, "You won't mention this to Monty, will you, Miss Starnes? I cannot think that he would approve."

"I should think not!" she exclaimed. "No, your brother has enough to keep him awake at night. I shan't add to it by telling him his twin brother is engaged in something so daring and unethical." Kicking Snowdrop, she cantered away.

"Daring and . . . Wait a minute!" When he had caught her up, he said, "I understand daring, but unethical? I would say that is rather harsh."

Glancing up at him, Clarissa asked, "And what would you have done if Thunderlight had tripped and gone down? What would you have done if you had lost another man's horse?"

Max shifted in the saddle, looking decidedly uncomfortable.

"I had not really considered the possibility."

"Well, consider it now. It could still happen."

At this, Max brightened. "No, it could not. Now that I have the money, I would buy him back."

"And if the winner did not wish to sell him? What would you tell the Marquess of Cravenwell?" She rode ahead and a moment later, he appeared by her side again.

"You are no slow top, Miss Starnes."

"Why, thank you, Mr. Darby."

"Too bad Monty cannot see clearly at this moment. I would much prefer to have you for a sister than your cousin, if you don't mind my saying so."

Clarissa gasped, and then exhaled slowly. "No, Mr. Darby, I do not mind your telling me that, but please, do not tell your brother. He is doing what he must do, what he wants to do. We should not question him on his choice," she said, her breathing shallow and difficult.

"If you say so, but I still say he is a fool," he replied. "Well, I really should get Thunderlight back to the mews. Needham will be wondering what has become of us. Good day, Miss Starnes."

"Good day, Mr. Darby," she said, waving as he rode away. "They make a wonderful team. He's a magnificent beast, isn't he?" she commented to her groom who rode up beside her.

"A magnificent fool," said Mitch.

"I was talking about the horse," she said repressively.

Clarissa returned to the house and climbed the stairs to her room to change. She had just removed her habit when the door flew open, and Adele marched into the room.

"What am I to do, Rissa?" she wailed, throwing herself on the bed and sending the old cat flying.

"Whatever is the matter?" asked Clarissa, trying to keep the contempt out of her voice.

"It is Papa! He has decreed that I must choose a husband by the end of the month! That is only two weeks away!"

"Then you must simply choose," said Clarissa, trying to coax the cat out from under the bed.

"Of course I must, but which one? I had thought Mr. Darby would be the perfect one, but after last night's exhibition . . ."

Clarissa straightened and glared at her cousin. "Last night's exhibition? The poor man did nothing except wear a suit of armor to please you because you had begged and wheedled until he agreed to do so. Then, you were not content to merely sit out a dance with him. No, what must you do but force him to try to dance. If there was any exhibition last night, it was merely an exhibition of your temper and selfishness."

Adele burst into tears. Between the loud sobs, Clarissa could make out several phrases that made her heart turn to ashes.

"You are right! I am a beast!"

"No, you are not a beast," said Clarissa, handing Adele a handkerchief.

"I am, and I am selfish, too. I just could

not help myself. I wanted to see how much he would do to please me."

"You got a bit more than you bargained for this time, didn't you?" said Clarissa.

Adele blew her nose and continued, "I . . . I just wanted him to prove how much he loves me."

"And are you now satisfied that he does?" asked Clarissa.

"I . . . I suppose so, but Rissa, I do not think he will come back — not after the way I yelled at him."

"Yes, he will," came the flat reply.

"Perhaps not. There are only two bouquets of flowers this morning and one of them is for you!" said Adele, amazement over this fact coloring her tone of voice.

Ignoring this, Clarissa said, "Perhaps he has not had time to send his flowers yet."

"But what is worse than that, have you seen the morning scandal sheets?" asked Adele, holding out a crumpled piece of paper. "Papa showed them to me when he gave me that awful ultimatum."

Clarissa knew, even before she smoothed out the creases, that it would be one of Tristram's wicked renditions. She braced herself not to laugh.

"It is not so bad," she managed to say.

Adele bounced off the bed. Looking over

266

Clarissa's shoulder she pointed to the picture. "Look closer. Look at my hair."

"Oh, my," said Clarissa, unable to prevent the tiniest giggle from escaping. "That was very unkind of him. Your hair doesn't look at all like snakes."

"It is not the way it looks, stupid. He is comparing me to Medusa. You know, the one in those Greek stories who had snakes for hair and turned men to stone when they looked at her."

"That would explain why Mr. Darby appears to be made of . . . stone," said Clarissa before bursting into gales of laughter. Apologizing with each breath, she lost control again when Adele thrust another drawing under her nose.

"I suppose you think this one is funny, too!"

Clarissa fell across the bed, silent laughter causing her sides to ache.

"Oh, I hate you!" screamed Adele before flouncing out of the room.

When Clarissa could control herself, she studied the second drawing more closely. "Wicked boy," she whispered as she gazed at the drawing, so like the one in her jewelry box, that depicted Adele as a spider with Monty and Lord Benchley caught in her web, struggling to get free.

Humphries hopped on the bed again, and she stroked his silky head and scratched under his chin while she allowed her mind to wander over the events of the morning. She felt a deep hollowness in her heart when she reviewed the conversations with her uncle and Maxwell Darby. It seemed that her uncle's ultimatum would force Adele to accept Monty's offer — an offer he had yet to make. She might have held on to hope, but Max's assertion that his brother had made his choice could not be ignored.

She simply had to accustom herself to the fact that Monty, her Monty, was going to wed her cousin. Shuddering, she wondered how she would ever grow accustomed to that fact.

Clarissa went to her door and turned the key. Returning to the bed and sweeping Humphries into her arms, she gave in to the tears.

She might not have Monty, but at least, she could weep in privacy.

Ten

Another twenty-four hours passed, another interminable, miserable day in which Adele refused to leave the house, making everyone else pay the price with her crying and moping. Clarissa did her best to stay out of her cousin's way, but inevitably, they would meet. She never knew if the Adele she encountered would be wailing and miserable or callously cruel.

Miss Anderson and her Aunt Frances were not immune to these attacks either. After Adele had insulted Miss Anderson's beaklike nose and her mother's wishy-washy advice, they turned to Clarissa for help, summoning her to her aunt's private sitting room.

"You must talk to her!" said her aunt, dabbing at red eyes with a scrap of lace.

"Please, Miss Clarissa," said the chaperone. "This morning, she told me I made the milk curdle. She is . . ." This placid lady shook her head and hurried out of the room.

"She has thrown a candlestick at the footman, shredded all the invitations, and dismissed Bates," said her aunt.

"Which Bates wisely did not agree to," said Clarissa. "I know Adele is intent on making everyone as wretched as she is, but I do not see what I can do."

"You are the only one she will listen to."

"She threw a piece of toast at me this morning," said Clarissa. "Cannot Uncle Clarence reason with her?"

"He does not even believe me when I tell him what she has done. You know what he thinks of her. She is a perfect little angel in his eyes, always has been."

"Surely he notices . . . no, I suppose he does not. He leaves before she arises in the morning and comes home only to change for the evening at his club."

"Yes, but he did tell me that he would be remaining at home tomorrow. He says he has a feeling that Mr. Darby is going to call and make an offer for Adele. I pray God he does," said the distraught older lady.

Clarissa's hand began to shake, and she rose, kissing the top of her aunt's head before hurrying out of the sitting room and down the hall to her own snug bedchamber.

She took two turns around the room before stopping by the window and staring outside, a sad smile curving her lips. It was here that she had watched him that first day, she thought. Here, that she fell madly in love without even knowing his name or his character. If only things had stopped there. If only she had not discovered that his character was the very best part of Montgomery Darby.

She had two choices. She could do nothing and allow things to continue as before. Or, she could speak to Monty and convince him it was time to act.

Clarissa was not at all certain that her uncle had the right of it. If Monty were still planning to make an offer for Adele, he would never have allowed the scandalous drawings to stem his intentions. He must know that the drawings were the work of his own brother and that Adele would be devastated by them. Surely he was not so green that he didn't realize Society was having a heyday over the fall of the belle of the Season. Perhaps he just needed to be prompted.

But could she bring herself to urge the man she loved to ask for her cousin's hand in marriage?

She cast back for that image of Monty as he spoke of his home, of Darwood Hall. The love in his eyes when he spoke of that place . . . She would have to let that guide her.

She would speak to Monty.

Looking up from his breakfast that same morning, Montgomery said, "Going out riding, Max?"

"What? Uh, yes, yes I am."

"Mind if I come along?"

"Well, Thunderlight is already at the door. I sent for him earlier," said Max, edging toward the door.

The clock began to chime. "Eight o'clock. I asked for Parsnip to be brought round at eight, too. I'll get my hat."

"Very well," said Max, kicking at the table leg with his booted foot.

They headed toward the park in silence. Max kept fidgeting in the saddle, and finally, Montgomery said, "Whatever is the matter with you this morning? You are making Thunderlight nervous."

"Yes, I . . . dash it all, Monty. Why did you have to come with me this morning?"

"What is that supposed to mean?" demanded Monty, stopping his mare and frowning at his twin. Max clamped his lips together and scowled back.

Glancing down the road to the park entrance, Monty saw two men on horseback.

They waved, and he looked at Max, who was shaking his head. The men started toward them.

"You might as well tell me the whole, Max," said Monty. "They will be here in a minute, and I don't think you want me asking them what is going on."

"Blast you, Monty. Nothing is going on. That is . . . everything is fine, really."

"Hey, Darby, don't tell me you are going to forfeit," called one of the men on horseback.

"I have to do this," said Max, urging his horse forward. "I'm coming. I still have five minutes."

Monty followed, his frown deepening as he listened to their conversation.

"Yates is champing at the bit. He really thinks that big gelding o' his can beat Thunderlight."

"Impossible!" declared the other young man.

Monty gave Parsnip a little kick and came abreast of the trio. "Are you not going to introduce me, Max?"

"You have already been introduced," he growled.

"Ah, yes, at Lord and Lady Forsyth's, the night the pleasure barge went down. A pleasure to meet you under better circumstance, gentlemen." Giving a little chuckle, Monty added, "I hope these may be better circumstances."

"No doubt about that, Mr. Darby," said the one called Callahan. "Yates will never be able to beat Max."

"Never," murmured Monty, spearing his brother with a raised brow. "Tell me, is it too late to get in on the wager?"

Max snapped, "No, you can't. . . ."

"I don't know," said Callahan. "We usually just bet horses, not money, since none of us are very plump in the pocket these days."

"Horses?" said Monty, bringing his mare to a halt and staring, his mouth hanging open.

"Now, Monty . . ."

"Have you got windmills in your head?" roared Montgomery. "What you are doing is illegal!"

"No, it ain't," said the young man who had been silent up to now. "It's quite all right. Oh, I don't say I enjoyed having to buy back my own horse, but Max here was very generous, so I . . ."

Montgomery silenced him with a look and said, "Max, might I have a word with you in private?"

"Don't know that there is enough time," said Callahan.

"Then we will make time," said Montgomery, using his horse to separate Max from his foolish friends.

"Monty, if I am not there at the appointed time, I must forfeit. You cannot wish for that to happen. I . . . I'm not at all certain that Yates will sell Thunderlight back to me. He breeds horses, and . . ."

"Now I know you have lost any sense you ever had. You have been racing a horse that doesn't belong to you, and the wager has been for that same horse, who still doesn't belong to you!"

"And will not, if I don't hurry," said Max, maneuvering Thunderlight around the mare. "I have no choice. We will talk later," he said, urging the stallion forward.

Monty shook his head and followed. Yates was older than the others, perhaps forty years. He was short and spare, and rode a huge gray gelding with a deep chest and powerful haunches. Monty tried to catch Max's eye, but his brother was all business.

"One time around the edge of the park, as agreed, gentlemen," said Callahan, raising a handkerchief in the air. "Ready! Set! Go!"

Monty leaned forward in his saddle, cheering Max on at the top of his lungs.

Whatever mischief Max was involved in, he knew that winning this race was vital.

Neck and neck, they disappeared in the trees. Hearing the rattle of a carriage, Monty looked over his shoulder and gave a quiet curse.

"Montgomery, what the devil are you doing here?" demanded the Marquess of Cravenwell. "Didn't think you would approve of your brother's nefarious activities."

"I . . . I only just learned of them, my lord. I promise you, it will not happen again."

"Why not? I told the boy, as long as he was careful to race only the ones he could beat, and as long as he split the winnings with me, he could race all day long, every day."

"You knew about this?"

The dry cackle was drowned out by the sound of hooves as Max and Yates reappeared. "Not at first, but once I found out, you can be sure, I was not going to let the young scapegrace off the hook. He's managed to repay me at least a tenth of what you Darbys owe me. More than I can say for you. Now, if young Tristram would use his talents to blackmail these people instead of just selling his drawings to the scandal sheets, I might die a rich man."

"I . . . I don't know what to say."

"Say nothing. Here they come. Come on, boy! Use the whip!"

The horses whizzed by, their hooves churning up the green grass. Callahan let the handkerchief drop as Thunderlight passed by first, a mere nose ahead of the big gelding.

"Max did it again!" shouted Callahan.

"Good for him. Tell him to come see me later," said the marquess, giving his driver the signal to go.

Grinning, Max came trotting up on Thunderlight with Yates following more slowly.

"We did it again!" he said, patting the stallion's neck.

"How fortunate," said Montgomery, turning his horse toward the gates to the park.

"Monty, wait!" called Max. "Good race, Yates. You can pay Callahan. I have to go."

He turned the stallion and followed Monty out of the park. When they had ridden for several minutes, Max said, "I guess you spoke to the marquess."

"I did."

"So you know that I have his blessing."

"Oh yes, as long as you win. And what

about before he found out about this?"

"Well, that was different. That was just me and some of my friends, having a lark. There was never really any danger of us losing," said Max, giving his horse a confident rub.

"He says you have been paying him back the money that Papa lost to him."

"You know about that, about him threatening to throw Papa into debtor's prison?"

"I had guessed that that was why he was paying for our visit to London," said Monty dryly. "I never believed he was doing it out of friendship. I daresay the marquess does not even know the meaning of the word."

"Oh, he is not so bad. I mean, he is rather blunt, but he was happy to let me continue racing, even after Needham had confessed the whole to him."

"Oh, so it is not enough that you wager a horse that doesn't belong to you, you also endanger the position of a trusted servant."

Max frowned, but he did not reply. After another few minutes of silence, Monty heaved a heartfelt sigh.

"It seems none of us have accomplished what we set out to do. Though I must admit, you, with your foolish wagers, and

Tristram, with his fiendish drawings, have managed to do more than I have."

"But Monty, I thought you were ready to offer for Miss Landis."

"I had planned to do so. I don't know. What with the scandal over Tristram's drawings, and the scene at the masked ball — not that I really blame her for being angry over that, mind you. The time just doesn't seem right."

"I suppose not. Still, from what I understand, Miss Landis is quite an heiress. Her fortune could fix everything. And they do say that her father has been overheard at his club, complaining about her fickleness. Might be a good time."

"Perhaps," came Monty's noncommittal reply.

"So we are no longer at odds over my, uh, activities?"

"No, Max. As long as you have Cravenwell's blessing, who am I to quibble? Go ahead and enjoy yourself."

"Thanks!" said his brother, whirling his big stallion around and heading back to the park.

Monty sagged in the saddle, and he turned his horse in the direction of Westminster Bridge. As the buildings thinned, he felt the weight of the past few weeks begin to lift from his shoulders. It had seemed such a simple plan in the beginning — not that he had given it much chance of success, not with it being his father's idea.

Then they had arrived in London, and since the very first day, he had been single-minded in his pursuit of Miss Landis. His prize. Oh, he had guessed that she was spoiled, and he had liked the idea of being there to spoil her. She was beautiful and stylish, and so at home in this setting that was as foreign to him as . . . the moon.

He had been delighted to discover that she would provide both a fortune and a loving wife, all rolled into one. What could be more perfect?

In his mind's eye, a face with golden-brown eyes and a pert nose mocked him, and he kicked Parsnip, unwilling to listen to her. No, he was merely feeling blue-deviled, what with Tristram's drawings and Max's foolish escapades. He had found the perfect wife — a lady he could love who would one day possess the wherewithal to turn his beloved Darwood Hall into an estate they would all be proud of.

Monty smiled, looking around him at the open countryside. How he longed to implement some of the new farming methods he had read about. And land. He would buy back the land that had been sold off. And for Max and Tristram, he would see to it that their homes were as grand as they wished.

Smiling, Montgomery Darby turned Parsnip toward home. He would send a message to Mr. Landis immediately, asking for an interview. In a day's time, everything would be settled.

"Adele, may I speak to you for a few minutes?" said Clarissa, poking her head into her cousin's pink room.

"About what?" said the voice from the bed.

Clarissa crossed the soft carpet to look down at her cousin, who was lying across the bed, her eyes puffy and red.

"Your mother asked me . . ."

"My mother is a prattling fool," said Adele, sitting up and glaring at Clarissa. "You know it, and so does everyone else."

"You should not talk about your mother that way," said Clarissa.

"Why? Because she did not have the decency to drown at sea like yours did?"

Clarissa slapped the splotchy cheek without compunction. Adele gasped and then fell back on the bed, covering her

281

head with a pillow, sobbing with all her might.

"I am sorry," said Clarissa, keeping her voice even with some effort. "But Adele, there are some things you simply cannot say. Do you understand?"

She didn't know if her cousin would sit up fighting or crying, but she was relieved when it was the second. Sitting down on the edge of the bed, she opened her arms, and her cousin flew into them, sobbing and apologizing for her behavior.

When Adele had recovered sufficiently, Clarissa wiped her tears as if she were a child. "Now, now, I know you did not mean it. Tell me, Adele, what can I do to help?"

"No one can help me!" came the dramatic response. "Papa has . . ."

"Yes, I know about the ultimatum, but surely you are ready to choose between Mr. Darby and Lord Benchley."

"Lord Benchley has withdrawn his offer," said Adele, in a little girl voice. "And I have not heard from Mr. Darby since that awful masquerade ball. What am I to do, Rissa?"

"Oh, I see. I did not know about Lord Benchley."

"Papa called me to his study this morning, before going out for the day. He told me that I must accept Mr. Darby or be sent home in disgrace."

"But you said yourself, Mr. Darby has not called or . . . anything since the ball. How does your father think you can accept a man who has never offered for you?"

"I . . . I told him Mr. Darby had hinted that . . ."

"Adele, how could you dare?"

"I thought there would be no harm, and Mr. Darby has been so very particular in his attentions toward me."

"Before the ball," said Clarissa, trying to keep her cousin focused on that important point.

"Yes, yes, but Papa knows that Mr. Darby is a pauper, or as close as it gets to that, and he has told me that he will settle an entire estate on me when I wed. Not only that, but he has promised me my very own house right here in London so that I shan't have to dwindle away in the country."

"And if Mr. Darby wishes to live at Darwood Hall?"

"Darwood . . . what is that?"

"His estate in Cornwall."

"Cornwall? Oh, I would never live in Cornwall. I suppose we might visit it once a year, but I could never live in such a backward place!"

As she spoke, Adele's spirits rose, until she was smiling and chirping as if Monty had already offered for her. Clarissa felt her own spirits falling in contrast.

"No, we will live here in London. He may go and do whatever he needs to do during the year. In the summer, of course, when it is so very hot here, we will live on the estate Papa has purchased near London. That way, I may come to the dressmakers or the theater whenever I wish."

"So you have it all planned out."

"Yes."

"There is only one problem, Adele. Mr. Darby has not offered for you."

Seconds passed while a transformation came over Adele, turning her cheery smile to a horrible grimace. Tears welled in her eyes, and she said tightly, "I think you are the most horrid person in the world to remind me of that, Clarissa Starnes!"

"I am only trying to point out the flaw in your plans."

"Flaw? There wouldn't be a flaw at all if . . . never mind about that." Frowning fiercely, Adele appeared lost in thought for several seconds before her brow cleared.

"You! You must go to Mr. Darby and tell him he has to offer for me!"

"Me? Me? I will do no such thing!"

"But it will be easy," said Adele, clutching at Clarissa's sleeve. "He likes you. He will listen to you. And you must tell him about the estate near London and the town house. He is poor, that cannot help but impress him."

"Adele, I cannot do this. I . . . I do not have the audacity that it would take to do such a thing!"

"But you must, Rissa, you must. How else am I to find my way out of this coil? And only think, Rissa. You will be doing Mr. Darby a favor."

"And how do you calculate that?"

"You said yourself that he loves this Hall place. You can tell him that Papa will give him the money to fix it up any way he pleases. Why, for all I care, he can move it, stone by stone, onto the grounds of our estate near London. Tell him that. That should induce him to make an offer for me."

"Adele, I cannot possibly go to his home. I shall be ruined."

"Rissa, please! For my sake and Mr. Darby's, too. Besides, you don't have to go to his rooms. Send a note around to him

285

and ask him to meet you somewhere — Gunter's tearoom, for example. Surely there can be no harm in that!"

"He may not be at home," said Clarissa hopefully. "I cannot wait at Gunter's all day."

"Pleeease," wheedled Adele. "Surely you will not deny me this one favor."

"Oh, very well. I know I shall regret this, but I will meet Mr. Darby at Gunter's, and I will speak to him on your behalf."

"No! You mustn't let him know that I asked you to do this. If he thinks that, he will think me desperate."

"But you are desperate," said Clarissa.

"But he mustn't know that. He mustn't be that sure of me. You must simply tell him that you want him to offer for me, that you think it is the wisest course of action."

"Oh, very well. Anything to have this conversation end," said Clarissa, prying her cousin's hands from around her neck and slipping out of the room.

Going to her own room, she sat down at her dressing table, gazing at herself and shaking her head. Staring back was a young lady of quality who looked as if she had been through a battle. Her smooth chignon was a thing of the past, and her eyes held a hunted look. If this was what it meant, being a good friend to her cousin and to Mr. Darby, then she had had quite enough of it.

She took out the pins in her hair and picked up the brush, taking long, even strokes. Finally, she replaced the pins and rose, going to the basin and bathing her face. After drying her hands, she inspected her dress and decided to change into something more suitable. She was unsure what one wore when trying to snare a bachelor, but if she was going to face Mr. Darby, she wanted to look her very best.

When she had changed into a dark gold carriage dress, she started down the stairs. In the hall below, Adele was waiting to give her some last minute instructions.

"Remember," she whispered. "Do not let Mr. Darby know that I have sent you."

"I shall remember."

"Good." Adele started to go up the stairs, but paused on the first step and asked, "Do you have that sapphire necklace you borrowed last week? I thought I would be wearing something suitably modest, like my blue morning dress, when he calls."

"Yes, it is in the bottom drawer, on top of my jewel case," said Clarissa before heading for the front door. Porter threw it open and waited, but Clarissa stopped suddenly, her face losing its color.

"Oh, no!" she exclaimed, pivoting on her heel, picking up her skirts, and heading for the stairs. At the landing, she stopped when an ear-piercing scream rent the air.

Porter and the footmen were on her heels as she sped toward her room. Her aunt and Miss Anderson had poked their heads out of the sitting room and watched with interest.

Clarissa skidded to a halt at her door, then dropped her head and closed her eyes, wishing she could make time turn around and undo the last few minutes. She was aware of Porter closing the door, giving them privacy.

"I am sorry," she said, walking forward and taking Tristram's original drawing from Adele's limp hand. For once in her life, her cousin was silent, and her silence cut through Clarissa's heart like a knife.

"How could you?" said Adele, staggering away from her and sitting down on the bed.

"I didn't want you to find this," said Clarissa, joining her cousin on the bed.

"Why would you do such a mean, callous thing to me?" said Adele.

"Do? No, no, I didn't draw it. Tristram gave it to me."

"Tristram? Mr. Darby's funny little brother? He is the one who drew those awful pictures of me and sent them to the newspapers?"

"Yes, though he didn't mean any . . . harm . . . either," said Clarissa, the untruth of her statement making her fall silent.

"Oh, and no harm was done, was it? I mean, my reputation is in tatters. My suitors have all fled. You knew about this and you did not stop him. I can never forgive you."

"Adele, I said I was sorry. I did not think Tristram would sell those drawings. I thought he had more sense."

"He has probably poisoned his brother's mind against me, too. You could have prevented all this," said Adele, her eyes narrowing as she watched Clarissa. "It is up to you to fix it."

"How can I fix this?"

Adele snatched the drawing out of her hand and scurried to the door. "When you go see them, you must get this Tristram to one side and tell him that he can make up for what he has done by helping you convince Mr. Darby to offer for me."

"I cannot do that. I have no influence

at all with Tristram."

"But you must. Why else would he have given you this," she said, shaking the drawing at Clarissa. "Between the two of you, you will be able to convince Mr. Darby."

"So I am to send a message asking both of them to come to Gunter's."

"No, we cannot take the chance. Papa is expecting Mr. Darby to call in the morning. You cannot waste time sending notes. You must go directly to his lodgings and see him there."

"Adele, I will be ruined."

"And if I show this to Papa, you will be without a home, not to mention that Mama and Papa will be so very disappointed in you."

"You would not dare," said Clarissa.

Adele smiled sweetly and said, "You know that I would. Now run along. There isn't a moment to lose." Adele opened the door and waited for Clarissa to pass, holding the drawing behind her back so she could not tear it out of her hands.

"I don't care what you say, Monty, I will not apologize. I cannot abide Miss Landis. Anyway, she has no idea that I was the artist behind those drawings."

"Don't blame him. The few times I have clapped eyes on Miss Landis, she has been a frightful bore," said Max.

Ignoring this comment and glaring at his youngest brother, Montgomery demanded, "Do you not care that you have harmed someone's standing in Society?"

"And what was she trying to do to your standing in Society when she insisted on your making a fool of yourself at that masquerade?" asked Tristram, throwing out his chest and glaring right back.

"Excuse me, Master Montgomery, but a young lady has called," announced Barton, his face the picture of shocked incredulity.

"I'm leaving," said Max. "Called for the curricle and team some five minutes ago. They should be here soon enough, and I have no desire to be caught up in this."

"I am leaving, too," said Tristram. "I refuse to stand by and witness your demise at the hands of that termagant."

Clearing his throat, Barton intoned, "Beg pardon, Master Tristram, but it is not the, uh, termagant, but another young lady."

Montgomery frowned, and said, "Well, do not keep her standing on the threshold, man. Show her inside, and quickly. As for you two, go ahead. I don't want to listen to your . . . good God! Clarissa! What the devil are you doing here?"

Montgomery went to her immediately, leading her to the sofa and sitting down by her side. Still holding her hands, he asked, "Whatever are you doing here, my dear girl?"

"I . . . Adele . . . I mean . . . I have come to ask you to . . ." She could manage nothing further. Her throat seemed to be closing up, and she coughed, the sound closely mimicking a sob. Tristram and Max, who had been watching this spectacle from the doorway, rushed to her side, too.

"What can we do to help, Miss Starnes?" asked Max.

"Do not cry, Clarissa," said Tristram.

Looking into their handsome, concerned faces, Clarissa could no longer hold back the tears that had been threatening since leaving Adele. The tears began to flow, and three serviceable handkerchiefs were thrust at her, and Monty began his usual two-pats-at-a-time rhythm on her shoulder.

"Do something, Monty," said Max, backing up a pace when the tide of tears seemed to be growing in strength.

"What would you have me do?"

"How should I know? You're the one

292

who knows all about chasing the ladies."

"Shall I get you some water?" asked Tristram, rising from his kneeling position in front of her. Clarissa shook her head, and he, too, retreated.

"Get out of here, both of you. I will take care of Miss Starnes," growled Monty, putting a proprietary arm around her shaking shoulders.

"Psst! Monty, a word, if you please," said Max.

"Will you be all right, Clarissa? It is just like Max to choose this time to speak to me."

She waved a hand and managed a brave smile.

Max's version of a whisper was deafening as he said, "Are you crazy? You cannot have a lady in your rooms, especially alone like that."

"Even I know that," said Tristram.

"And what do you suggest I do with her? Turn her out into the street?"

The three men grimaced, staring at Clarissa until she turned away. Finally, Max snapped his fingers and said, "Take the curricle. It should be here by now, and it's the racing curricle, a little tricky, but I think you can just manage it."

"And do what? Parade her through the

park?" asked Monty.

"No, go for a drive in the country. Just do not stop, not even for a moment, not until you are clear of the city and anybody who might recognize either of you," said Max.

"You may have something there. Stay with her a moment while I put on my boots."

Max and Tristram edged toward Clarissa until she turned and said, "Boo!"

Her eyes were still red from crying, but she had a smile on her face, and they visibly relaxed.

"Glad you are feeling more the thing, Miss Starnes," said Max.

"Very glad," echoed Tristram.

"I am sorry to be such a watering pot," she said. "I assure you, I am not usually such a ninny."

"You're not a ninny at all," declared Tristram. "You are a real Trojan. If only Monty could see that."

"You are too kind," she murmured.

"It's a shame Monty left his good sense at home," said Tristram, nodding toward Montgomery, who had just returned to the room.

"We are going for a drive, Miss Starnes," said Monty.

Clarissa didn't speak, but allowed him to whisk her out of the bachelor apartments and into the waiting racing curricle. After climbing in after her, he tapped the leader with his whip, and off they went at a good clip.

As Montgomery navigated in and out of the traffic in the late afternoon sun, he stole glances at her from time to time. Clarissa kept her eyes straight ahead, reveling in the pleasure of riding by his side. If she looked at him, she would feel compelled to fulfill her promise to Adele.

When they had left most of the houses and other buildings behind, Montgomery heaved a sigh of relief and slowed his team to a mere trot. "I must tell you, Miss Starnes, should you ever again find yourself in a similar situation, do not do it."

"Do what?"

"Do not ever visit another gentleman's lodgings. It simply is not done. If anyone saw you entering or leaving this afternoon, your reputation will be ruined."

"What if I have a very good reason for visiting this gentleman?" she asked innocently.

Montgomery brought the team to a complete standstill before giving her his full attention. "I cannot think of any reason you should ever have for visiting a gentleman's apartments, Miss Starnes."

"But you have not yet heard why I visited you today," she replied, gazing up at him and wishing he could see how unfair he was being.

"It does not matter," came the ponderous reply. "You were wrong to have done so, no matter what the circumstances. You should have sent me a note if you wished to speak to me."

"And you would have replied, and we would have set a time and place, and finally, when it was too late, we would have had our little chat," said Clarissa, folding her arms and staring straight ahead.

Lifting the ribbons and once again giving his team the office to start, Monty began to chuckle. It was an infectious sound, and Clarissa, who had been so recently on the edge of despair, began to laugh, too. Before long, Monty had to stop the team again, as their hilarity made driving impossible.

Just as they thought they had regained their composure, they would look at each other and fall into whoops again.

Recovering slightly, Clarissa said, "I can just see us at Gunter's tearoom, with me sobbing my eyes out and you patting me —

twice each time — on the back."

"Here now, what is wrong with that?"

"Nothing. It was at least as effective as Tristram offering me a glass of water. Tell me, have you ever known a glass of water to ward off a flood of tears?"

This caused him to chuckle, and he said, "Having only brothers, my experience with floods of tears is decidedly limited."

In complete charity with each other, Monty set the horses to a steady trot and said casually, "I shall enjoy having you as part of my family, Clarissa."

Clarissa's heart skipped a beat, or perhaps it had stopped altogether. "Part of your family?" she repeated slowly.

"Yes, assuming your cousin accepts me," he replied. "I sent a note to her father, asking for an interview tomorrow morning."

"So he was right," murmured Clarissa, as her amusement fled, and a coldness settled over her. Her voice void of any emotion, she said, "I feel certain she will."

"Do you really think so? I have been doubtful, since the masked ball, if she really wanted anything to do with me."

"Oh, yes, she does. As a matter of fact, you will be delighted to know that, despite his finding out you are a penniless fortune hunter, Uncle Clarence has decided to buy you a town house, as well as an estate near London, in addition, I should imagine, to the usual settlements, dowries, and such. Congratulations."

Bringing the team to a halt once more, he set the brake and turned to face her. "But that is good news."

"Yes, excellent news. You and Adele will have everything you have ever wanted."

"Yes, I suppose we will," he said, looking down at the tears filling her eyes and frowning. "Clarissa," he whispered.

She looked into those brown eyes, took a deep breath, and threw her arms around his neck. Let him tear her away from him in disgust. She could not remain in his company another minute and not be in his embrace!

His lips found hers, capturing them for an eternity as their arms wrapped around each other. Seconds later, his breathing ragged, he tore his lips away, kissing first her cheek, then her ear, and finally, resting his chin on top of her head, still holding her as if he would never let her go.

Clarissa gave him a squeeze, before relaxing her embrace and moving away a few inches to look into his eyes.

With a rueful grin, Monty said, "I don't

suppose you have some money hidden away in an old stocking."

"Oh, Monty," she said, the tears returning and starting to fall — faster and faster until he could not kiss them away quickly enough.

"Do not worry, love. We will manage. We still have Darwood Hall."

"Darwood Hall! Oh, Monty, you cannot possibly marry me. Your beloved Darwood Hall will fall down around your ears."

"And my father will be in debtor's prison," he said with a mirthless chuckle. Shaking his head, he grinned at her and said, "What do I care, as long as I will have you, my sweet Clarissa?"

"But Uncle Clarence was going to give you the money to fix up Darwood Hall, to turn it into a showplace. And for Max and Tristram, too. I . . . I cannot do this to you."

"You cannot? Of course you can, and you will! Do you think that, now I have realized I love you, that I am going to let you go?" His dark eyes glinting with anger, he sent the horses cantering down the country lane before wheeling into the stable yard of a small, neat inn.

After handing the team over to a groom, he held up his arms to help her down, swinging her easily to the ground and into a quick embrace. Holding her hand, he led her inside.

"Have you a private parlor, landlord?" he asked.

"Yes, sir. Right this way," said the owner, leading them to a small, snug parlor with a decent fire and a small sofa in front of it.

"This will do just fine," said Monty. "Could we get some tea and a little something to eat?"

"Certainly, sir," said the landlord, catching the coin Monty threw his way.

Monty led her to the sofa and sat down by her side. He pulled out his pocket watch and glanced at it, putting it between them on the cushion.

"What is that for?" asked Clarissa.

"That is to remind us of two things as we talk. First of all, that time is fleeting, that life is precious, and we must do that which will make us happy."

Clarissa smiled at him. Shaking her head, she asked, "And the other thing?"

"The other thing, my dear Clarissa, is that we have about two and one-half hours of sunlight left today. If we talk longer than two hours, we will have to wed anyway because I will not have time to return you to your uncle's house before dark."

"Monty, what I feel for you, and what you may feel for me, it is not the sort of thing people of our class should base a marriage on."

"Are you telling me, Clarissa Starnes, that you do not think marriage should be based on love? My father may be a wastrel, but I know he loved my mother until the day she died. I expect to do no less for the lady I love."

Clarissa's breath caught in her throat, and she found speech impossible for several seconds while he grinned at her.

Then, shaking her head, Clarissa said, "What I think, dear Monty, is that if you offer for Adele, you will have everything you ever wanted — two estates, a house in town, a beautiful wife. . . ."

"The only thing I have ever wanted was Darwood Hall, and I have that. If you are willing to take it and me as we are . . ."

The landlord entered with a heavy tray and placed it on the small table in front of the sofa.

"My wife makes an excellent kidney pie, sir. I do hope you and your good wife like kidney pie."

"That's fine," said Monty. He flipped another coin to the landlord and said, "Would you see that we are not disturbed.

We are on our honeymoon, you see."

"Honeymoon? Then I will make certain you are left alone, sir. Congratulations! The missus will be that proud, knowing her kidney pie is serving as your wedding feast. Just let me know if there is anything else. Should I make up the best chamber, sir?"

Clarissa and Monty said in unison, "No!"

Blushing, Clarissa said, "We are not actually wed yet. We are on our way to be married."

"Oh, it'll be Gretna Green for you then?" When she nodded, he said, "It's not so bad. The missus and me, we ended up there because her father was always against me."

"Really? And how many years have you been wed?"

"Almost thirty now, miss. So you see, there's naught wrong with being married over the anvil."

"Yes, well, your wife's excellent kidney pie is waiting," said Monty, and the landlord finally left them in peace.

"Gretna Green," he said. "Wherever did you get such an idea?"

"Perhaps it is because I know that our alternative is to return to my uncle's house and listen to Adele's angry tirade. What is worse, I would deserve it."

"You do not. You cannot help it if I have finally come to my senses and chosen you over her. If she yells at anyone, it should be me," said Monty.

"Do not worry, my love. She will," said Clarissa, reaching up with her napkin to dab away a bit of pastry clinging to his lower lip. "Of course, if I do not go back now, when I finally do, she will probably have taken scissors to all my gowns."

"Surely she is not so bad as that," said Monty.

"Is she not? Do you know why I came to your lodgings?" asked Clarissa.

"I assume it was to encourage me to offer for your cousin."

"Yes, but the reason I came there instead of sending for you is because she threatened to tell Uncle Clarence that I had betrayed her, that I had sent that drawing to the scandal sheets."

"Surely you do not think your uncle would believe such a tarradiddle."

"I am afraid he might do so when she shows him the picture from my room. It is virtually a copy of the spider drawing that graced yesterday's scandal sheets. She found it this afternoon."

"How the deuce did you happen to have one of Tristram's drawings, especially that one?"

"I discovered him drawing them at the Forsyth's breakfast. I thought the one of Adele as a spider was too wonderful, and Tristram gave it to me."

"But that was two weeks ago. Tristram never said a word to me about disliking Miss Landis."

"He is very devoted to both you and Max. Tristram would never be so disloyal," said Clarissa, placing her hand over his. He took it and turned it over, kissing her palm.

"Oh, Monty, I have just thought. What about the letter you sent to Uncle Clarence asking for a meeting in the morning?"

"I forgot about that. All the more reason that you cannot go back tonight. This is what we will do. I will tell the landlord that we require two rooms."

"But the expense," said Clarissa.

"Do not worry about that. We will send a message to . . . Whom can you trust in your uncle's house?"

"I am sure that Miss Anderson and Porter would help me in any way they could."

"Good, then we will send a message to

them to pack some clothes for you. I will also send a message to Tristram and Max, telling them what we are doing and asking that they do the same for me. Tomorrow, when the messenger returns with our things, we will set out for Gretna Green."

"Oh, Monty, I cannot wait," said Clarissa, throwing her arms around his neck again.

The kidney pie grew cold while they sealed their love with kisses and sweet promises. Finally, Montgomery sat back, recovered his fallen pocket watch, and served their plates. They kept their conversation commonplace for the rest of the evening, but at her door, Montgomery could not stop himself from declaring his love once more.

"Are you certain about this?" he asked.

"Certain? I am ecstatic," she said. "I have loved you from the first moment I saw you, outside the Marquess of Cravenwell's house."

He smiled down at her and whispered, "I am sorry you are wedding such a muttonhead. It took me much longer to realize that you are everything I have ever wanted for a wife."

"I have decided to forgive you, my love. I might as well. I can hardly stay angry with

someone who makes my heart melt at the
very sight of him."

"I love you, sweet Clarissa."

"And I love you, my darling Monty."

Epilogue

"Masters Tristram and Maxwell, there is a person to see you, and he refuses to give me the message," said Barton, his nose in the air and quite out of joint.

"Don't worry about that, Barton. I'm sure you will find out what the message says in your own way. Send him in," said Max.

"Very good, sir," said the servant.

"I am surprised he could even reply, his lips were clamped so tight," said Tristram.

A young man of seventeen or eighteen stood at attention near the door, though his eyes roamed over the luxurious room.

"Well, hand it over, lad," said Max.

"I was to make certain that you are you," said the boy.

Max grinned at Tristram and quipped, "I am me; are you, you?"

"Stubble it," said Tristram. "Yes, I am Tristram Darby and this is my brother Maxwell."

"Thank you, sir. Here it is. I'm to wait."

"Of course," murmured Tristram as Max leaned over his shoulder and read the short letter.

"Huzzah!" shouted Max, startling the boy and bringing Barton running.

"So Monty finally came to his senses. Good for him," said Tristram. "It says he needs clothes."

"Right you are. Barton, pack up all of my brother's clothes."

"Master Montgomery's?" asked the servant.

"Of course, you dolt. Oh, and you should pack a few things for me. I'm going to drive them," said Max.

"You are not!" said Tristram. "Monty can manage quite well on his own."

"No, he cannot. The cattle he is driving are high-spirited. He'll never manage to get all the way to Scotland without ruining them."

"He is more likely to manage than you! At least he will not try to set a record for speed on the journey. No, he will do quite well on his own."

"But he won't be on his own," said Max with a leer. "He'll have Miss Starnes with him. He'll have his mind and perhaps his hands, on other things."

"Take that back!" yelled Tristram.

Barton cleared his throat. "Excuse me, gentlemen, but am I to understand that Master Montgomery has eloped with Miss Starnes?"

"That's right, Barton. Our big brother has landed himself a wife."

The servant's knees buckled, and he staggered to a chair where he held his head and began to moan.

"Devil take you, man! Whatever has gotten into you?" demanded Max.

"You do not understand, Master Max. You do not understand."

"Then tell us," said Tristram, handing Barton a large glass of whiskey.

The servant drank it greedily before speaking. "It is the marquess. He will have my hide when I tell him!"

"Then do not tell him," said Max.

"But I must! I have to report everything to him or . . . or he will cast me out without a penny!"

"What the devil are you talking about, Barton?"

"He . . . he caught me with his . . . paramour," said the servant with a shudder.

"Whew, that must have been unpleasant," said Tristram.

"Almost deadly. He sent her packing, of course, but I had been with him so long, he decided to find some way of punishing me without actually dismissing me."

"So he punished you by making you serve as our majordomo," said Tristram.

"That doesn't say much for the marquess's opinion of us."

"Oh, but it has been wonderful, sir. Serving the three of you young gentlemen has been a privilege. You are so forthright, so honest, such gentlemen. What a refreshing change for me! I have thanked heaven for you every night, but I was supposed to see to it that you wed heiresses, and I failed."

"Stiff upper lip, Barton," said Max. "We won't let the dirty marquess fire you. We'll smooth things over. Besides, Tristram has been paying him a bit of our debt and so have I, and I think the old man actually likes me. We'll smooth it over, never you fear."

"Oh, Master Max, I would be ever so grateful," said Barton.

"Think nothing of it," said Max, rocking on his heels feeling very pleased with himself.

Tristram raised a brow and said, "If we could return to the practical now? Monty's clothes, Barton?"

"Oh, of course. Right away."

The servant hurried into the bedroom and returned fifteen minutes later to find the brothers sharing glasses of port with the youth. The boy sprang to his feet when

Barton entered with the large portmanteau.

"Here it is. See that you do not open it or spill it."

"Let me have a look," said Max, rising and taking the bag back to the chair he had just left.

With his back to the others, he winked at Tristram and pulled a heavy purse out of his coat pocket. Poking the purse deep into the bag, he closed it and fastened it shut.

"Take good care of this bag, Luke," he said, handing it to the boy and patting his back.

"I will, sir. I promise."

"Thank you," said Tristram, reaching into his own pocket and pulling out several coins. "This is for you. Have you already been to the other house?"

"No, sir, I came here first."

"Come on, Max. Let's go with Luke to the Landis house. I will speak to Porter and enlist his aid. Should make things a great deal easier."

"Capital idea. Let's go!"

With Barton bidding them good luck, they hurried outside and to the waiting dogcart. Max squeezed in beside the boy and promptly confiscated the reins. Tristram threw the portmanteau into the back and hopped on top of it.

Having a rollicking good time, they sang as they rode through the darkened streets. When they reached Mayfair, they grew quiet, even going so far as to stop the dog-cart one house down from the Landis town house.

"You stay here, Luke. Max and I will handle this."

"Have you thought what you are going to say to Porter?" whispered Max.

"Not exactly. I mean, if he is reasonable, then Miss Starnes's letter will explain it to him and Miss Anderson."

"Well, knock softly, Tris. You do not want to disturb the entire household."

"I will, I will," snapped Tristram, placing one foot on the first step.

The door swung open, and they stared up at the tall butler.

"Gentlemen, may I be of service?"

They hurried up the short flight of steps and dragged the butler outside.

"Porter, it is Tristram Darby."

"Yes, sir. I did recognize you. And this, I presume, is your brother Maxwell."

"Yes, how do you do," said Max. "We have a letter from Miss Starnes."

"Very good, sir. We had begun to get worried," said the butler, holding out his hand. "I will be happy to give it to Mr. Landis."

"No!" they whispered in unison.

"The letter is for you and Miss Anderson. We will wait here while you give the letter to her, and then you can bring down the bandboxes."

"I am certain this all makes perfect sense to you, gentlemen, but I am afraid that is not how things work in a well-ordered household, and I assure you that my household is very well-ordered."

Max shook his head and said, "Porter, we appreciate your household being well-ordered, but this is a matter of vital importance to Miss Starnes and my brother."

"In short, they have eloped, and Miss Starnes needs your help," explained Tristram.

"Very well, sir. I will deliver this to Miss Anderson as soon as possible. Please realize, however, that things are a bit . . . tense this evening since Miss Starnes has gone missing. But I will do my best."

"Good man," said Max.

When the butler had disappeared into the house, Max took one look at Tristram, and they hurried to the nearest window. Max cupped his hands and Tristram stepped up high enough to peek inside the drawing room.

On the sofa, Clarence Landis sat with Adele, rubbing her wrist and speaking to her. Frances Landis was sitting in a chair, reclining almost to the point of lying down, her hand to her forehead, covering her eyes.

"There he is," whispered Tristram as Porter crossed the room, pretending to check the teapot which was in front of Miss Anderson. "He's signaling to her. She's getting up. Uh-oh," he added.

"What is it? What's happening?"

"He dropped the letter. There, he's picked it up. I don't think anyone noticed. No, I was wrong. Miss Landis has snatched it out of his hands."

"Hang onto the ledge," said Max, waiting only a second before releasing his brother and jumping up to cling to the windowsill, too.

The windows were closed, but they had no difficulty hearing what was going on.

Screaming at the top of her lungs, Adele Landis yelled, "Eloping! Eloping with my fiancé!"

"He is not your fiancé, Miss Adele," said Miss Anderson.

"He would have been if she had not

gone to his rooms and compromised herself, the little . . ."

"Adele! You mustn't say such a thing about your cousin," said Miss Anderson. "Now, I am going upstairs and pack some things for Miss Clarissa."

Screaming invectives, Adele ran at the chaperone, tearing at her hair and scratching her face.

"Adele, stop that this instant!" ordered Clarence Landis, grabbing his daughter and pinning her arms against her sides. "I will not allow you to behave in such a shocking manner, do you hear me? Go on, Miss Anderson. Porter will help you."

"You!" screamed the girl, tearing free and heading for the butler. Again her father caught her in his arms.

"Stop it!" he screamed, wrestling her onto the sofa and holding her there.

"He was supposed to be mine! I planned everything."

"Adele, you would not want such a man. I mean, a man who would lure a girl to his rooms and . . . compromise her," gasped her mother.

"Lure her to his rooms? I sent her there! She was supposed to persuade him to marry me, you stupid woman! I hate her! And I hate you, you foolish . . ."

Max and Tristram flinched as Clarence Landis's hand flashed across his daughter's cheek.

"Not another word out of you, Adele. Not another word!" said her father.

With this, he rose and held out his hand for his wife to join him. Together, they left their daughter sitting in shocked silence.

The silence was short-lived. As Porter directed the footmen to carry out a large trunk, Adele followed, flying down the front steps and into the street, screaming at poor Luke until she spied the Darby brothers.

Turning her ire on them, she grabbed the short whip out of the boy's hands and started swinging.

Doors started to open and onlookers peered out at the unusual sight of the well-dressed Miss Landis being carted off by her butler. Sobbing, the fight had been taken out of her, and she allowed him to return her to the house and shut the door.

The neighboring doors began to close. As Tristram and Max congratulated themselves on a job well done, a familiar voice broke the newfound stillness of the night.

"So he chose the right one anyway," said the Marquess of Cravenwell, shaking his head in disgust.

"Yes, he did," said Tristram.

"Pity. Shouldn't have let his feelings get in the way of business."

"I think they will be very happy together," said Max, his expression daring the old man to contradict him.

The marquess reached into his coat and pulled out a heavy purse. Pitching it to Max, he said, "You better saddle that horse of yours and ride guard over that boy." Turning, he made his way toward his front door.

"What is the money for?" called Tristram.

"What do you think it's for? A deuced wedding gift, you country rustic!"

With all the delays, it was almost dawn before the trio arrived back at the inn. Tristram had slept in the back of the dogcart while Max drove the marquess's new gig.

Their arrival in the yard caused quite a stir, and it wasn't long before the landlord and his wife were hovering over them in the private parlor, pouring coffee and serving up hot bread and melted butter.

"What are you two doing here?" demanded Monty, rubbing his face and squinting at them from the doorway.

"We have come to your rescue, Brother," said Max.

"I don't need rescuing," he replied, shuffling toward the table and sitting down. The landlord poured him a cup of coffee and hurried out, leaving the three brothers alone.

"You should have been there, Monty," said Max, rubbing his hands together gleefully.

"I thought I asked you to be discreet," said Montgomery, taking a sip of the hot liquid and then simply holding the cup, warming his hands.

"Why didn't you tell me we were having a formal breakfast?" said another sleepy voice. Monty hurried to escort Clarissa to the table. She motioned for them all to be seated again.

"What are you laughing at?" she demanded, giving her intended a kittenish glare.

"I would have said I didn't want my future wife to come downstairs in such a state of undress, but after seeing your ensemble . . ."

"It is the landlady's best nightrail and wrapper," said Clarissa, giggling despite her show of haughtiness. "Of course, it wraps around me twice and at least a foot of it trails along the ground after me. But it was very kind of her to lend it to me."

"Well, we've brought your own things, so you may change out of that whenever you wish," said Max.

"Have you? Oh, thank you, boys."

"Good heavens, she already sounds like our big sister!" exclaimed Tristram.

"And did you bring anything for me?" asked Monty.

"Whatever Barton packed," said Tristram. "Oh, and this," he added, opening the portmanteau and producing the purse Max had placed inside. "It's from Max."

"It's from both of us," said Max. "He just doesn't realize it yet. Better get busy drawing, Tris."

"Thank you, but I cannot take this," said Monty, pushing the purse back at them.

"Then you will be leaving the landlord a very big tip," said Max, pushing it back.

Clarissa and Monty smiled at each other, and he said, "Very well then. Thank you."

"Oh, and there's more," said Max, pulling out the marquess's heavy purse. "This is from Cravenwell."

"You stole it?" breathed Monty.

"Don't be daft! Of course we did not steal it. He was there tonight, when Miss Landis . . . well, I will tell that story later, with a great deal of relish. . . ."

"And embellishments," said Tristram.

"But what about the marquess?" prompted Clarissa.

"He said you're a fool, Monty, for choosing the right one, whatever that means," said Max.

"It means he knows our Clarissa it worth a thousand of her cousin," said Tristram. "And I quite agree, of course."

"Yes, yes, we both agree on that point," said Max. "But the crusty old man said that the purse is your wedding gift."

With this, Max poured the contents onto the table. All four of them gasped.

"Why, that sweet, wonderful, wicked man!" said Clarissa, tears filling her eyes.

Shaking his head, Monty smiled at her and said, "Who would ever have thought that old man could be so sentimental."

"Oh, Monty, I think I am going to cry again," said Clarissa.

"Now, now, no need for that, my love. You're still half asleep. Why don't you go back to bed?"

"I think I will. Good morning," she said, yawning as she rose and stretching mightily before leaning forward and kissing the cheeks of each of her new brothers.

"I think I am going to enjoy having brothers."

"Just wait until you get to know them better," said Monty, leading her from the parlor.

He accompanied her up the stairs and to her door, where he stopped, resisting the urge to go inside. He kissed her tenderly on the lips and she responded hungrily. Shaking his head, he sighed and put his forehead against hers.

"This is going to be very difficult, Miss Starnes, remaining a gentleman all the way to Scotland."

Clarissa licked her lips and whispered, "Just how long will it take to get to Gretna Green?"

"Too long, minx, but we will be strong, will we not?"

"Yes, very strong," she replied, kissing him once again before slipping inside her room.

As she peeked at him through the narrow opening, Monty said, "Just remember, my love, the sooner we arrive . . ."

"Have the landlord send up my case. I will be dressed and ready to leave in half an hour."

Laughing as she closed the door, Monty called softly, "I love you, Miss Starnes."

"And I love you, my dear Mr. Darby."

ABOUT THE AUTHOR

Julia Parks lives in Texas with her husband of thirty-two years. She teaches high school French and loves traveling to Europe with her students and family. When not teaching or writing, she enjoys playing with her grandchildren, quilting, and reading.

She appreciates comments from her readers and hopes you will contact her through Zebra books or via e-mail at dendonbell@netscape.net.

We hope you have enjoyed this Large Print book. Other Thorndike, Wheeler or Chivers Press Large Print books are available at your library or directly from the publishers.

For more information about current and upcoming titles, please call or write, without obligation, to:

Publisher
Thorndike Press
295 Kennedy Memorial Drive
Waterville, ME   04901
Tel. (800) 223-1244

Or visit our Web site at:
www.gale.com/thorndike
www.gale.com/wheeler

OR

Chivers Large Print
published by BBC Audiobooks Ltd
St James House, The Square
Lower Bristol Road
Bath BA2 3SB
England
Tel. +44(0) 800 136919
email: bbcaudiobooks@bbc.co.uk
www.bbcaudiobooks.co.uk

All our Large Print titles are designed for easy reading, and all our books are made to last.